THE INHERITANCE

Beyond Happily Ever After

THE INHERITANCE

Beyond Happily Ever After

BY
ADENA HODGES

Circumference Press

The Inheritance - Beyond Happily Ever After

Cover art by Bridgette Millar

Editing and layout by Circumference Communication
www.CircumferenceCommunication.com

ISBN: 978-0-9789229-7-9

Printed in the United States of America

To my beloved husband, Gil
and our three amazing children,
Caleb, Titus and Rebecca
Its all about the journey!

Acknowledgements

If you find any life in the book you hold in your hands, it is because of King Jesus to whom I owe the greatest debt of gratitude. I hope you discover His love speaking to you on each page.

This book would not be here in this form without my good friend, Suzy King, who took my raw version and brought color and personality to the characters therein. I can't thank you enough for the many, many hours of editing and re-writing but mostly for partnering with me in the process.

Many thanks to cherished friends who cheered me along this journey and gave me the encouragement to complete this project.

Huge thanks to my husband, Gil, for his loving support through the hours of writing. Thanks for your patience when your shirts weren't ironed or meals ready on time.

I'm grateful for my oldest son, Caleb, for helping with layout and design. Thank you, Titus, for cooking for the family when I was preoccupied with writing. And special thanks to my daughter, Rebecca, for reading the manuscript and sharing her thoughts with me.

I'm indebted to my mom, Jeanne Peters, for her encouragement, insight and ideas for this book. Thanks, Mom!

CHAPTER 1

D im light filtered through the grimy window, revealing the quiet attic for what it had become, a playground for spiders. The feeble beams illuminated their silken threads, intricately woven between rafters and walls, and generously spread over every surface. Entering cautiously, one hand up to protect my face from the trailing webs, I tugged on the yellowed pull cord dangling from the lonely 60 watt bulb, and prepared to take a closer look.

I'd optimistically expected this topmost room of the house to be filled with furniture, boxes, knick-knacks, and perhaps something of real value I could sell on EBay... but it wasn't. Rather than the treasure trove I'd envisioned, standing alone in the middle of the floor sat a battered old wooden chest of some kind. It stood about a foot high and maybe two feet wide, roughly the size of a tool chest. I moved toward it wondering what might be inside and felt the excitement of an adventure begin to tickle my imagination.

A week earlier, my mom had called to let me know my great aunt Annabelle had passed away. Even though

I'd only seen her on a few occasions, family reunions and such, I'd always liked her and her passing saddened me. Imagine my surprise when Mom informed me that Annabelle had left me an inheritance. The only catch being the 426 mile drive from our home in Grand Rapids, MI to Wheeling, OH to pick it up. She'd said, "Whatever is in the attic is yours, Ann."

I couldn't help wondering why this charming woman that I barely knew would leave something to me. Whether she had been "well to do" or not, I had no clue; however, the word "inheritance" conjured up images of wealth and riches. There'd been rumors of some royal connection to our family in the distant past and my imagination toyed with the possibilities. Could she have left me some antique jewelry? A rare coin collection? Priceless china? Surely it had to be something valuable if I had to drive all the way to Ohio to get it. I breathed a silent plea for this to be the reverse in fortune we were praying for. Oh, how we needed it!

Life for Mark and me had begun well enough, following in the footsteps of our parents who were well educated and enjoyed prestigious careers. Dating throughout college, marrying shortly after graduation, we embarked on what we thought would be a "happily ever after" life. Unlike some of our peers, we knew what we wanted and weren't afraid to work for it. I guess you could say we had big dreams, but why not? Nothing we wanted seemed beyond our reach.

Mark's engineering degree landed him a job right out of college with a prominent architectural firm. With a good position, he quickly began rising in the ranks. My master's degree in business administration opened the door for me at Dynatel, an up-and-coming Telecom Company. Life was perfect. With great jobs in careers we loved we felt confident that soon the rest of our dreams would turn to realities as well.

Owning our own home was at the top of our list. After a few weeks of searching, we purchased our first house. Though small, it delighted us with its idyllic charm. Someday we'd need something bigger, but until then it was the ideal starter home, complete with a white picket fence. Every weekend was spent fixing it up, transforming it into a place that was uniquely ours. We poured ourselves into making it "just right." From the assorted wildflowers planted near the front gate to perfecting the landscaping in the backyard, we left no detail unattended.

Next on our list was to find a church. Although we'd grown up in different denominations, we discovered a wonderful compromise in a midsized community fellowship - a place where we could continue our family traditions of faith and service. We soon fell into the routine of attending services on Sundays and occasionally volunteering in various church activities when our schedules permitted it.

"Comfortable" accurately described our lifestyle. All that we wanted or needed was at our fingertips, our destiny following the predictable path we'd planned.

The years passed and our salaries increased. It appeared the ideal time to expand our family. The exciting thought of having children and actually needing more room made the decision to sell our little cottage relatively easy. Scouting the suburbs became our new weekend passion as we searched tirelessly for the perfect place to put down roots and watch our branch of the family tree grow.

It took a little time, but at last we found a four bedroom house located in a beautiful new development, our dream home. "Only one block from a good school and park!" I thought with excitement, imaging pushing little ones in the swing or watching them fly down the slide.

The price of the spacious 2,700 square foot residence cost more than I felt comfortable with. Even though it met every criterion on our wish list and appealed to me in every way, I couldn't help feeling we were biting off more than we could chew. Though Mark tried to ease my mind with assurances that our current salaries could handle our increased overhead, I didn't actually give in until he exclaimed, "I was going to wait to tell you, but I'm getting a raise starting next week! I got the promotion! We can afford the house and start a family, too!"

The following months found me caught up in a whirlwind of decorating and furnishing our new home, all the while dreaming of children's happy voices filling these rooms in the years to come.

That first Christmas we invited Mark's family to our home for the holidays. Though they lived only three hours away, our busy lives didn't leave us much time to spend with them. Tom and Nelda, Mark's parents, arrived first. Giving them the grand tour, they appeared delighted with the new house and neighborhood. Impressed with the way our lives were going they congratulated us on "moving up" in the world. Nelda even complimented me on my taste in décor.

Mark's sister and her husband, Missy and Jack, also expected for the family get-together, arrived a short while later. They'd barely stepped inside the door before surprising us all with the happy news that they were expecting their first child in July. Missy, full of her own tidings of joy, barely noticed our new home seemingly oblivious to the improvements we had labored lovingly over for months. As we toured the rooms she followed along blithely describing every doctor visit and proudly showing off the first ultrasound pictures.

Though genuinely happy for them, the constant baby talk became a painful reminder of the months we'd been trying without success. I understood her excitement; if it had been me I would have been just as ecstatic. But it wasn't me. I couldn't wait for them to leave as it seemed every conversation between us had become a chance for her to get one-up on me. They had a bigger house. Their jobs were better. Theirs would be the first grandchild...

Eventually the question arose as to when Mark and I were going to start a family. My ever confident husband answered brightly, "We hope soon to fill our home with youngsters." I wanted to stay optimistic about it, but I finally confided to Missy how long we'd been trying without success.

I suppose I had hoped for compassion or at least some consideration, but she thoughtlessly blurted, "Really? You better call your doctor. Seriously, you should've been pregnant by now! I conceived right away." It felt like an accusation.

That conversation stuck with me, and as I replayed it in my mind, my anxiety increased. What if she was right? What if there really was something wrong? The next morning I called my doctor for their earliest available appointment, but was disappointed they couldn't get me in until the following month. Ah, the waiting game. I thought our local drugstore would run out of pregnancy tests I'd bought so many of them over the last year. How much more of the crushing cycle of anticipation and disappointment could I take?

Finally, the day of the doctor visit arrived. Grateful Mark had taken the day off from work, we nervously scanned the Parenting magazines on the coffee table in the waiting room anticipating our turn. Eventually, my name was called and after the usual preliminaries, Dr. Bradstone performed all the typical procedures. I breathlessly awaited his verdict. Leaning back in his chair he said, "Can't see any reason for trouble, but we'll have to get further tests before giving my final answer."

This buoyed my spirits. I just hoped it wouldn't end in frustration and I hated the idea of more waiting, but it appeared inevitable.

Four long weeks passed before we found ourselves impatiently seated again in the reception area. When at last we were taken to the exam room, I tried to read something into the nurse's face. She seemed cheerful and upbeat. Maybe it would be a good report or something that could be easily remedied.

"I'm sorry, the news isn't good." With that first sentence I sensed an end to our charmed life. My doctor, a very compassionate man, wasn't one to give false hope. "I wish there was something I could do to help, but even with expensive infertility treatments it will be nearly impossible for you to get pregnant."

No! How could this be happening? My dreams and hopes of becoming a mother vaporized in an instant. My fairy tale over, my heart crushed. I don't remember much Dr. Bradstone said after that, my shock and pain overwhelming me.

Silence filled the car on the ride home. Mark reached for my hand, trying to console me, but the tears just came harder. At home I busied myself with various tedious tasks, trying to block out the doctor's words, "impossible." Finally near midnight, Mark insisted I come to bed. Laying side by side, an icy wall seemed to grow between us. It was my fault. I'd let Mark down. Accusations filled my heart. Where was God? He made me this way. Did He even care about me?

Trying to break through the unspoken barrier between us, Mark reached out for me, "We can always adopt."

I recoiled from his touch and words. I couldn't even think about it. I knew he meant well, but just suggesting it told me he had no idea of what I was going through. He didn't seem to understand that I felt broken inside. I wanted to have a baby with my own body and that dream had just been shattered.

I spent weeks grieving as I mourned my loss, occasionally feeling guilty for the pain I knew I caused Mark by my distance. How could he understand? Depression's ugly hand beckoned me, and in the haze of pain I was completely unaware this was only the beginning of our troubles.

Mark looked pale and shaken as he came through the door that awful night several months later. I'd never seen my husband so distraught. Wordlessly, he handed me an envelope containing a single page of paper. His two weeks' notice. "Laid off." The words hit me like a two-by-four. I felt the cold hand of dread squeeze my heart. "How could this happen?" I demanded, even as I regretted my accusing tone. Trying to soften it, I reached for Mark's hand, "What happened, Honey?"

When Mark finally found his voice, he explained that the crashing real estate market had hit his firm hard. Over-extended in their speculative investments they had to let people go to avoid bankruptcy.

I hadn't realized things were so bad. Between my preoccupation of our new home and the emotional fall-out from the doctor's report, I'd pretty much ignored the news about the downturn in the economy. Assuming our jobs were secure I thought we had nothing to worry about. Now, hard reality hit home.

Like a revolving door, the question "How could this be happening to us?" churned through my mind. We'd only been in our beautiful house a little over a year, and it took both of us to keep it going. Sure, we had a little savings, but it wouldn't last long with Mark's hefty salary gone. "What about my own job?" I thought. Oh Lord, what would happen if I got laid off, too? What a nightmare! If only I could just wake up and find us back in the wonderful American Dream!

Somehow we limped through the next couple of months. Mark relentlessly looked for another engineering job, but with little success. Occasionally he'd seem to get a nibble of a possibility here or there; but whenever we allowed our spirits to rise, disappointment would crash in as each new lead hit a dead end.

Swallowing his pride, Mark began looking for any job available. Though willing to work anywhere, I couldn't imagine my talented and well educated husband flipping burgers. On the bright side, as long as my job held out we could get by on his unemployment, but not without dramatically cutting back our lifestyle. No more dinner cruises on Lake Michigan, and kiss those Mackinaw Island getaways good-bye! With a humorless chuckle I imagined date night dinners under the neon lights of a fast food sign rather than the soft glow of candles I had become accustomed to.

My heart broke watching the life slowly drain out of my husband as he fought hard to keep us going. When Mark gave up the lease on his Lexus and bought a used Ford I knew my car would be next. I know it sounds silly, but I loved my Audi and kept praying God would intervene somehow.

More and more I found myself wondering where God fit into the equation? Our circumstances were becoming increasingly desperate. It just didn't seem fair. We'd done all the right things. We'd been faithful in our tithing, and we rarely missed church. How could He let all this occur? Day after day worry clouded my thoughts. Night after night my head whirled vainly through all the "whys." Though I kept thinking it couldn't get any worse, it did.

Four months later my supervisor called me into his office and shut the door. My stomach flip flopped. This couldn't be good. "I'm sorry, Ann," was all he said as he handed me my pink slip. I wanted to get on my knees and beg for my job back, even part time, but I knew it was pointless. Though the accompanying letter assured me it was due to the economy, I couldn't help feeling somehow it was my fault, as I hurriedly cleared out my desk.

Depressed, the following Thursday, I watched as they took away my Audi. My "new" beat-up Volkswagen was so ancient it had an AM radio and cassette player in it. How embarrassed I felt to even park it in front of our house. But I had a sinking feeling it wouldn't be an issue for very long.

We tried to hold on, but living on unemployment couldn't pay for our dream home. Within a few short months we lost everything. Devastated, I said good bye to my co-workers, my job, my car, my home and my dreams of a family. The future I had built my hopes around now completely gone. Smashed like castles in the sand. Demolished with little hope of recovery.

Eventually, Mark found a job painting houses, which paid him less than unemployment. But what did it matter? The unemployment would run out shortly anyway. I spent my days searching for a job and keeping house in our one bedroom apartment. It had been advertised as "cozy" – definitely an overstatement. We had to sell or give away much of our furniture to be able to fit in these close quarters.

On Sundays we attended our old church, but it now felt as lifeless as my womb. Being unemployed gave me more time to volunteer and it seemed like the right thing to do, but it left me drained and unfulfilled.

Now here I stood in an empty attic looking at a decrepit chest hoping it contained a miracle. Wondering if it would even be worth the effort, I fished the old key I'd received from the lawyer out of my pocket and gingerly inserted it into the lock. The creaky hinges protested as I lifted the lid and stared down at...nothing. Empty! This was my inheritance? What a cruel joke! I couldn't believe I'd driven all the way here for naught.

Slamming the lid closed, the images of the trunk's barrenness reflecting the aching void in my own heart. Sitting down hard on the wooden floor, ignoring the billows of dust rising all around me, I pondered our fate. Like a slap in the face when you are already down, it was just too much. Another slim thread of hope snipped in a second. I sat staring at that worthless chest as the tears began to fall. Finished...the dream was over.

At last, giving my pity-party a break, I mindlessly turned over the tag on the trunk and read, "Annabelle." Oh, how I disliked that name! Annabelle. So old fashioned. A family name, but oh, how I wished someone else had gotten it. Through grade school I'd endured the taunts of children who knew just exactly how to twist a name to tease a body to tears. By my teens I had convinced my parents to let me go by "Ann" but it didn't seem to fit me either. So here I sat, alone with the only two things that I shared with my great aunt... a name and an unfilled chest.

A decision had to be made. I contemplated just leaving this useless coffer of unfulfilled promises here in the attic, but somehow I couldn't quite bring myself to just walk away. My temper rose as I contemplated the waste of time and money I'd expended, both of which were in limited supply, just to come here for nothing. In frustration, I kicked the trunk hard and watched it tumble and slide across the attic floor.

I would have left then, but I thought I'd heard a noise...a slight rattle or scrape as if it contained something more. Running to it, I carefully turned it upright imagining I perceived the sound again. But opening the lid only revealed what it had before--nothing. Could it be just a trick of this creepy attic or my imagination?

Fearing to hope again, I teetered between walking away and investigating further. But curiosity won the battle. Opening the chest again, I felt around the inside. Worn velvet lined the chest, more regal appearing than I'd first thought. In the dim lighting I couldn't quite tell what color it was, but the faded fabric might have once been royal blue. In examining the dimensions more closely, I noticed that the interior looked too small, as if there might be a false bottom or maybe a secret compartment.

Once again hope and excitement surged through me. Maybe, just maybe, treasure lurked somewhere hidden inside. I turned the box around checking carefully for a concealed latch or lever to open up the hidden compartment I guessed must exist, hearing once again that slight rustling noise. Finding nothing on the outside, I pulled open the lid to search the inside again.

At first, I couldn't see anything out of the ordinary, but something caught my attention and I felt a little like Sherlock Holmes as I spied one corner of the velvet lining pulled slightly away. Giving it a gentle tug revealed another keyhole hidden beneath. With trembling hands I fumbled the old key again out of my pocket and breathlessly inserted it into the lock. A reassuring click rewarded me. I reached inside to carefully lift out the false bottom revealing the secret compartment.

This had to be it; the hiding place of the treasure. The moment of truth had come. Holding my breath I opened the secret compartment. As my eyes at last gazed upon my aunt's final gift to me, my heart plummeted. The fortune I'd envisioned turned out to be nothing more than a thick packet of letters, yellowed with age and tied with a gold ribbon. A post-it note on the outside read simply:

> *To Annabelle.*
> *Enjoy your inheritance.*
> *It changed my life.*
> *It can change yours.*
> *Lovingly, your*
> *Aunt Annabelle.*

How could this packet of letters change my life? What I needed was a job, or to win the lottery, or an inheritance that would at least bolster our shrinking bank account. In short, I needed something of real value... something I could use. What difference could some ancient words on a page make in our desperately declining circumstances? Another dead end was more than I could take.

Ah well, I resolved to deal with reality. If the letters were as fragile and old as they looked, further investigation would require much better light and the right environment. Besides, I still had the long drive back ahead of me. I wanted to get on the road before it got too late. No money for a hotel and I certainly didn't want to sleep in this spooky attic. Weary and disheartened, I placed the packet of letters back in their hiding place, loaded the chest into my old Volkswagen, and began the long journey home.

Watching the highway signs slide by, I concluded searching for a happy ending to our troubles had come to a dead end. Better to live in survival mode than repeatedly have my hopes raised up just to be dashed by the bitter sting of disappointment.

For now I had 426 long, silent miles stretched out ahead of me to ponder what fate had brought me. There'd been no miracle to save us from our present crisis. No help to pay the rent, and no way to recoup the expenses of a wasted trip I wished I'd never made.

As I tried to focus on the road and put the disappointment of the afternoon behind me, I found myself entertaining a fragment of interest in the back of my mind. What was so special about these old letters? What did they contain? Perhaps they unveiled some family mysteries, or related the tale of a secret romance. Whatever they held, they might at least offer a diversion from the long fruitless hours of searching for a job.

Exhausted both physically and emotionally, I arrived home at last. "Home" seemed too inviting a word to use for our cramped apartment filled with second hand furniture and left over dreams. Definitely not the "happily ever after" I'd imagined when Mark and I got married eleven years ago.

Mark met me at the car. Reading the disappointment in his eyes about our lackluster inheritance, I asked him to put the trunk in the corner of the living room until I had a chance to look at it more closely.

When I'd called him on the drive home, I could hear his initial excitement die away into silence as I described what I'd found. Now as I watched him evaluate the plain chest, it was obvious he considered it merely another piece of sentimental junk to add to our mismatched furnishings.

Mark smiled obligingly but I knew he was trying to put on a good front and spare my feelings. I could almost hear him thinking, "Lost letters? That's not going to put food on the table."

Two days went by with me playing the "catch-up" game after my trip, but now the curiosity that had been niggling in my mind about those letters finally surfaced full force and I found myself kneeling at the trunk, carefully unlocking the secret compartment and drawing out the delicate communiqués.

I sat back on the sofa with the little bundle on my lap, admiring the gold ribbon that encircled the packet. Holding the top one, I gently opened the well worn envelope and gazed at the ancient letter in my hand. The script was difficult to read, particularly in places where it was smudged or worn away with time. I wondered who had written it and how many hands had held it as mine did now.

The first words "Dearest Annabelle" caught me off guard as I stared at my own name. But then, remembering the mysterious bits and pieces of our family history, I realized this letter wasn't really addressed to me or even my great aunt, but probably to some distant relation.

Dearest Annabelle,

My beautiful goddaughter, while it may be some years before you can read these words yourself, I wanted to set out an account of my life for you in a series of letters so that when you are older you will come to know me for who I really am, not just some fairy tale version of myself.

Though the years have been kind to me, they have at last taken their toll and I expect my time here is nearly done. Someday you will discover how swiftly time passes and how, near the end, one can feel there is still so much to accomplish. This very sentiment leads me to share my journey with you, in the hope you will gain wisdom and understanding for your own journey. It is always best to hear a person's story in its entirety, and therefore, even though you will likely have heard some of my early story, I will begin my tale at the beginning.

I was born a princess, beloved of my father and mother who were the king and queen of a small kingdom not all that far from here. We were so happy in those days... that is, until my mother died suddenly and the whole kingdom was plunged into grief.

Being very young when it happened, I cannot remember a great deal about those days except that suddenly my whole world fell apart. The nobles thought it would be easier for us if my father remarried quickly, but this would prove to be the greatest mistake of his life. The woman he chose, though beautiful on the outside, was evil to her very core. The tragedy of my mother's death, and then his deep remorse for marrying this evil woman, wore away at my father until he too died and I was left at the mercy of his widow.

My stepmother stripped me of everything familiar, subjecting me to slavery. Jealous of the love my father and his subjects lavished upon me, she detested the purity and innocence of my heart. She, consumed with vanity, begrudged my youthful face and form believing my very appearance posed a threat to her. In her hatred, she tried every way she could to destroy me.

Rags replaced my beautiful dresses, and I slept atop a pile of straw on the floor instead of my soft bed of down feathers. Stale bread and water became my daily fare. I learned quickly that if I did not instantly obey her every whim I would be beaten, starved, or both. Yes, a very hard life, but I still remembered a time when I had known love, and thought maybe I would find it again, if only I could endure.

Years went by and I grew into a young woman. I tried to make each day as bearable as possible, often dreaming of escape and of a different life. Most of the time restrained inside the stone walls of the castle, only occasionally, when necessity demanded, did my stepmother allow me out of doors. One day, with no other servant available, my stepmother ordered me outside to draw water from the well.

This delighted me. Not only would it allow me a breath of fresh air, it would also give me the chance to see beyond the castle wall to the beautiful woods, and to hear the birds sing. Their voices were so bright and happy I found myself singing too. A song unfolded from my heart as I lost myself in imagining a handsome prince coming to take me away. All of a sudden, there he was, seated on a white horse and dressed in the finest clothes. I stared at him in awe and wonder. Was I dreaming or was he real? Then I heard his voice call to me, "My beloved, my beautiful one."

He was real! He was calling to me! Love and longing rose in my heart, but fear clouded my mind. There I stood, dressed in rags as a slave, with fewer means than a beggar. What could he be thinking? Surely he must not mean me? Ashamed of my appearance I ran away as quickly as I could. He called after me repeatedly, but fear drowned out his words.

I cannot say for sure that my step-mother heard him, but immediately thereafter her attitude changed toward me. That night she eyed me closely as she *plied me with many questions, and then locked me in my room. I cried myself to sleep that night and prayed I would dream of my prince.*

At that time I had no knowledge of my stepmother's magic mirror, but perhaps you have heard of it. She would stand in front of it gazing at her own reflection and ask, "Mirror, mirror on the wall, who is the fairest one of all?" Until then she had always been delighted by the mirror's response, but on that day it replied, "You are fair my queen but Snow White is fairer still."

My mind reeled. Seriously? My inheritance - a pile of letters written by a deluded woman who believes she's a princess from a fable? I threw the letter down in disbelief. Of all things! Love letters would have been much more interesting, I thought, besides I knew this fairy tale – happily ever after...blah, blah, blah. I'd had enough of that.

I would have left it there, but after a few moments, considered the only other things I had to do were job hunting and cleaning, neither of which were particularly appealing. Maybe this could be an amusing distraction for the moment, I thought, picking it up again.

The rage of my stepmother knew no bounds. Even had I known about her mirror and what it had said, I would not have anticipated her fury. I might have wondered why the looking glass had betrayed me, and wondered even more why she would be so jealous of me? After all, I was of no importance, just a rag clad slave. But I knew nothing of this event being fully ignorant of my danger.

The next morning when she sent me out into the woods with the huntsman my excitement knew no bounds! I had never been this far beyond the castle wall and longed to see the woods, the flowers, and the animals. The huntsman appeared gruff and grave at first, and more than just a little scary; but soon my happy chatter softened him and he began to tell me about the creatures of the forest as well as many other new and marvelously interesting things.

As the afternoon wore on, he grew silent and then sad. At last he sat down heavily, sighed deeply, and haltingly revealed the truth to me. He had been ordered to kill me because of my stepmother's jealousy. He told me about his daughter, a girl my age, and he reminisced about the happy times when my father was the king. At last he made up his mind and with a stern but gentle look he bade me run away as fast and as far as I could because he could not bring himself to harm me; but before he let me go, he warned me never to return or the Queen would kill me.

Terror filled me as I realized I must leave him and the only home I had ever known behind. Where would I go? What would I do? What if my stepmother found me? I ran and ran, tripping, and falling, and getting up again until I felt my heart would burst. I knew I had to find somewhere to spend the night as the sun slipped behind the hills. Just as my hope neared exhaustion, I found a tiny cottage in a clearing. It appeared empty, but could it be safe? Nearing collapse, my need overcame my fear. I went inside and fell immediately asleep curled up on one of the little beds.

How much time passed, I know not. Only that I awoke to find many rough faces peering down at me. I jumped up so quickly that I bumped my head on the low ceiling. Gratefully, these were not the faces of the queen's searchers. I feel sure you have already guessed who they really were - the seven dwarves, of course.

I told them my story and they agreed to help me and allowed me stay.

In truth, it looked as if they could use my help, too. I noticed the dirty dishes and the floor needed to be swept. Dust and grime covered every surface. I must have been too weary to notice the un-made beds the night before, but now they spoke volumes. The filthy pile of laun-dry generated by seven sweating, hard-working dwarves almost rose to the low ceiling.

My relief at having a safe place to stay made the chores easy to accept. I knew what needed to be done. Many years of scrubbing floors and dishes, laundry and cooking certainly qualified me for the tasks presented before me. The next morning the dwarves went off to work in their mines while I stayed at the cottage to clean and cook, and then clean some more.

Those funny, tiny men were proud they had rescued me. They liked to tell their friends how I "got saved" but to be honest, as the weeks went by there were times I felt that I was back in the castle, slaving away just to earn my keep. I hope you understand that I am not complaining when I say this, it is just the way I remember it. In truth the dwarves were wonderful, and each of them had his own special quirks and foibles.

Let's see....there was Fixit, the most vocal of them all. He carried a parcel of his "treatments" wherever he went. His specialty consisted of handing out bandages and lots of advice. He believed he knew just what everyone else should do, and he took responsibility for making most of the decisions for the others. Whenever anybody was sick or hurt he knew just which remedy was needed, and if all else failed, he always had a binding cloth at the ready. You might be wondering if anyone was ever really helped by his bandages. It makes me smile to remember it, but many said they got well in spite of them.

One of those who failed to recover from Fixit's treatments was Sneezer. He suffered from severe allergies. He seemed to be allergic to almost everything, and when he would sneeze...watch out! You could get drenched by the resulting spray. The constant sneezing and sniffling made him very disagreeable as well. Whenever something didn't go exactly as he thought it should or someone annoyed him, he would find any willing passer-by to tell his troubles to and then, kerchoo! The listener found himself drowned in a flood of foul words and saturated in muck. Very unpleasant indeed!

Snoozy also reaped no benefit from Fixit's abundant advice or topical cures. No matter what Fixit tried, Snoozy would just sleep through it. The only effect stimulant potions ever had on him was a momentary jolt, which resembled him being stung by a bee, followed by a long, deep slumber. Though unmoved by Fixit's treatments, Snoozy's yawning and snoring had a big effect on those around him. Anyone in close proximity would soon become drowsy, so the other dwarves insisted he work alone in the mine and he generally made little progress between extended naps.

Then there was Merry. The perfect name for him because he consistently radiated happiness. That should be good, should it not? It is certainly a wonderful demeanor to have... But, he appeared so happy all the time that, on occasion, it felt just too much to bear. It mattered little whether you were sad or angry, hurt or anxious, his ready reply was, "Don't worry. Be happy!" So convinced he was that any problem could be solved by simply deciding to be happy that his very presence could make you feel guilty if you were unable to comply. And this attitude made Grumbly even grumpier.

Dear old Grumbly. He had a way of being a dark cloud over every picnic. He would say, "It will rain today." And it would rain. He would say, "A wolf is going to try to catch us on our way to the mines." Sure enough, the wolf would come. His gloomy words proved true so often that the others felt he was cursed and was somehow causing the bad luck by his pronouncements. This caused most to fear him and keep their distance.

Everyone but Dimwit, that is. He seemed unaware of his fellow dwarves' opinions, and was one who forged his own path. "Dimwit," though not his given name, suited him best. "How did he get such a name?" you might ask.

Long before I met him he spent time with a band of unusual men who were traveling around the realm speaking in a strange language and exclaiming to all they met about the benefits of imitating them. They claimed that by uttering an incomprehensible language a person would become more spiritual, and gain a wisdom that others could only wish for.

So excited about what he learned, Dimwit began to mimic them, and he enthusiastically regaled the other dwarves with story after story expounding all the benefits of speaking in this "new" tongue. At first his fellows were curious and willing to listen, but as time went on and they saw no helpful changes in his life, beyond speaking what sounded to them like nonsense, they dismissed him as a lunatic. Fixit dubbed him "Dimwit" and the nick-name stuck.

The last and, some say the least, is Timorous or Timmy for short, the invisible one. Timorous was well... timid, and that made him a bit of an enigma. Outsiders thought him painfully shy. His brothers were always seeking the approval or at least the attention of everyone around them as they advised or tattled, slept long or danced, grumbled out warnings, or spoke gibberish.

Timmy neither wanted nor seemed to need the attention of others; he was content to just be part of the crowd; a spectator. If asked, he would lend a hand, but he was not one to volunteer or get involved. His ability to disappear into the background made him easy to miss, and hard to talk to. But when he thought he was completely alone, he would sing like an angel. Once while walking through the woods I caught him unaware. His song was, oh so sweet, the birds fell silent to listen. And when the birds resumed their songs, he clapped his hands and waved his hat about in the most wonderful way. Had he known I spied him, he would never have acted in such a manner. Timorous was hidden deep beneath his quiet manner, and determined to stay there.

Every day the dwarves would go off to the mines looking for treasure, and every night they returned home dirty and tired. I never actually saw them bring home anything of great value, and I often wondered why they worked so hard. Where was their treasure?

As for me, I cooked meals for my little friends, and worked diligently to keep the tiny cottage clean, beds made and laundry done. For the most part I felt happy. Great was my gratitude that they had saved me; but during the long hours they were away I often felt lonely, fearful and unprotected. Had my stepmother forgotten about me? Did she know I still lived? Would she try to find and kill me?

Fear began to eat away at me like cancer, but I had no one to talk to. Knowing the dwarves so well I could easily imagine what each would do if I went to them with my troubles. Fixit would offer advice or try to find a way to bandage me. Grumbly might tell me my stepmother knew where I lived and was on her way to get me and then it would come true. Merry would sing some foolish song about smiling my troubles away. Dimwit would spout gobbledygook at me and tell me to repeat it three times a day to become, "Right as rain!" I didn't want to get soaked by Sneezer's foul spray, or find myself nodding off to the sound of Snoozy's snores. Timmy left me feeling like I was talking to myself.

Just when it looked as if my fears would trap me forever, my life took an unexpected turn.

On an unseasonably warm morning, I took the wash bucket out into the yard to enjoy the sun and watch my woodland friends play as I worked. Just as I finished the laundry an old woman came out of the woods carrying a basket filled with shiny globes of red. Though hideously ugly, her soothing voice enchanted me as she showed me the beautiful apples she sold from house to house.

"Dearie, you look mighty tired. Why don't you sit down? Let me get you a dipper of cool water," she gently intoned.

I acquiesced, sitting down on a nearby bench. As I sipped the refreshing liquid, she surprised me further by offering me one of her apples. "Here, Beauty, take an apple, sweet as honey, my gift to you."

Not being accustomed to receiving presents of any kind, I was overwhelmed by her kindness. I knew the dwarves cared for me, but they were so busy looking for treasure that they seldom asked after me. When they did, it was usually a prelude to a request such as, "Snow White, how was your day and what are we having for dinner?"

The seemingly genuine attention from the old woman pleased me and I accepted the fruit. Oh the foolishness of it all! Being so preoccupied with my fears and worries about what I would do if my stepmother found me, I never even considered she might come in disguise. Without a second thought I took a bite from that crimson apple. You know what happened next.

Just as a deep, cold, unnatural sleep overcame me, my stepmother revealed herself with a mocking laugh, "I have you now, Snow White!" Horrified, I sank into oblivion.

Time was meaningless to me. How long I slept, hours or weeks, months or years, I was insensible. My poor dwarves were frantic. Fixit used every potion and bandage he knew of, but they could not stir my deep slumber.

Word spread that Snow White was dead, and as soon as the news reached the prince I had first seen in the court-yard, he mounted his white steed and came at once. I am sure you know more about that time than I do. All I recall is the feel of his kiss followed by warmth flowing through my whole body, and then suddenly feeling more alive than I had ever felt before. I opened my eyes to find him looking at me with such a deep love that I knew I could never be the same.

He proposed immediately, and our whirlwind romance soon turned into the wedding of the age. What a wonderful tale, and this is where I imagine you might be expecting me to say, "And we lived happily ever after." Right? Hmmm...not quite. For this is really just the beginning.

There is so much more to tell, but this letter has grown long, and I must *at last give in to my exhaustion. So, my precious Annabelle, more of the story will have to wait for another day, another letter.*

I remain, your loving Godmother,

Snow White

Great! Just what I needed! I could hardly believe what I'd just read. Aunt Annabelle had said her life had been changed by reading these fairytales, but I couldn't imagine how. What did magic mirrors and silly dwarves have to do with reality? Was my great aunt insane to think some children's tale could have an impact on my life? I closed the lid of the trunk and tossed the letters onto the coffee table.

What a worthless waste of time! I told myself to throw the ridiculous things away, yet somehow I couldn't do it. Even if I kept them I still didn't feel I could tell Mark about what they contained. It would only add insult to the injury of the worthlessness of my "inheritance." I went to bed that night with a heavy heart, and tossed and turned for what seemed like hours before finally falling into a restless sleep.

CHAPTER 3

After four days I still wondered why I hadn't thrown the faded letters away. Still lying on the coffee table exactly where I'd left them, they seemed to mock me and I felt myself getting a little angrier...silly old fairy tale! Mark and I lived in the *real* world and I had to face the cold, hard facts of life. There was no magical Prince Charming going to ride to the rescue on his dazzling white steed. No. My "prince" worked hard every day just to bring home scarcely enough to sustain our barebones lifestyle.

The following Sunday I found my mind wandering as the pastor droned on about storing up treasure in Heaven. Hmm...treasure...dwarves. Yes, maybe I could relate. I'd learned a bit about working hard and having little to show for it beyond the hope of glory somewhere "way beyond the blue" in "the sweet by-and-by".

Glancing around me, I spotted Mr. Carlyle contentedly snoozing - his usual pastime during the sermon and it kind of reminded me of...Snoozy. A smile formed on my lips.

I peeked behind me and saw Mrs. McPherson. Although appearing congenial, I tended to avoid her. If you wanted to know anything about anyone, she would be the person to ask. She had plenty of details, almost overly eager to share them and quick to give you her opinion when something didn't sit well with some issue or person in the church. Encounters with her often left me feeling kind of slimed. Sneezer, is that you? I actually chuckled. How long had it been since I'd found anything remotely humorous to giggle about? Enjoying this immensely, I looked around wondering if all the "dwarves" were here today.

I looked to the left where Mr. Coleman sat, always full of the "perfect" piece of advice and/or the solution to any problem. Just like "Fixit" he confidently believed that his approach to anything was the right way.

To my right, and a couple of rows up I saw "Miss Sunshine" Tabitha Lynn, constantly bubbling over with glee. Though it seemed genuine, her incessant cheerfulness almost made me feel sick. Yep, that's Merry.

But how would I find Dimwit? I really didn't get the whole "speaking in tongues" deal. With my conservative background I'd heard about charismatic churches, but I'd never been to one and I doubted I would find a "move of the spirit" like that here. Then again...Mr. McCormick could get pretty zealous during worship, sometimes raising his hands and shouting "hallelujah." Maybe that fit.

I couldn't decide who would make the best Grumbly, Widow Daniels or Dr. Kendrick? Both appeared as if they had just eaten sour grapes, or maybe caught a whiff of something stinky. I stifled another giggle.

As we stood to sing the closing hymn Mark gave me a "What's so funny?" look, but I just shook my head still looking for one more dwarf. Then I heard it, a tenderly sweet voice standing right next to me. Michael O'Shay, a youngster in his early teens who wore thick glasses and stuttered. I had seldom heard him say more than two words at a time, but here he was, eyes downcast, yet singing with the heart and voice of an angel. Well hello, Timmy!

How about that! All present and accounted for. I nearly laughed out loud. I felt a little guilty about my wayfaring mind that morning, but at least thinking about the "dwarves" seated all around me made the sermon go by quickly, and before I knew it we were glad-handing with our neighbors and heading home.

After lunch Mark took a nap, leaving me some alone time. Staring again at the letters, I wondered if they were worth another look? My aunt had found some significance in them, but would they actually have something meaningful to say to me, or would they just bring more disappointment? Finally, deciding that at the very least I might find something amusing in them to get me through next week's sermon, I picked up the next envelope, turned it over and withdrew the tattered page.

Dearest Annabelle,

Let's see where, was I... Ah yes, a charming Prince, a kiss, romance and a wedding. Most people end my story right here with "they lived happily ever after" and in many ways we did, but there is so much more to it than that. I felt genuinely happy. Mine the original "rags to riches" story. Shortly before we married, my Prince was crowned King and ascended to the throne. After our glorious honeymoon we returned to live in his castle where he desired me to rule as his queen. What a beautiful life! My King loved me so much and sought to show me at every turn. I enjoyed gorgeous clothes, fine foods, a soft bed, and every other comfort I could yearn after. For a time it satisfied.

Each day I donned beautiful robes, but on the inside I still felt like I wore rags, or at least that I deserved them. What was I doing to deserve all these fine things? I began to feel uncomfortable. What could I do with my time? Accustomed to working hard from sunrise to sunset, now with servants to wait on me I had little to do.

One day I could stand it no longer and went through my things until I found some of my old clothes. They were just rags really, but I put them on and went to work. Somehow I felt more comfortable scrubbing the castle floors then lying around in all the finery.

I made sure to finish my work and change back into my gown before my King came home that night. I hoped he would not notice the scratches on my hands from the rough floor or the bits of dirt under my broken nails. When my King asked about my day, I blushed and tried to change the subject. He merely looked at me with love in his eyes and said nothing.

After that I fell into a routine; as soon as he would leave for the day I would change into my old clothes and find some hard task to do around the castle. The work made me feel better, as if I deserved the rich foods and elegant clothing because I had earned it. I expected the servants to do exactly as I wanted because, after all, I had done some of their chores, so now they should jump to serve me. What I had not considered was the way my daily toiling would affect my treatment of them.

At dinner one night I snapped at one of the maids for some minor offense and then immediately regretted it when I saw the sorrow on my King's face. Later as we prepared for bed, he took my hands in his and tenderly traced the marks my hard labor had caused them. Gently he asked me what had happened. I made some excuse but found I could not look in his eyes as I assured him I would find some balm to put on them in the morning. With a small nod of his head, he gently kissed my hands and left it at that.

The next day I tried to rationalize my actions. I told myself that the King should be proud of me for working so hard and not taking advantage of his kindness. I earned my keep... This should be a good thing, should it not? But in spite of everything I tried to make myself believe, I found I could no longer enjoy the great pleasure I had once found in the company of my King. I began making excuses to be occupied whenever he arrived home.

My hands became so rough and dry that I began to wear gloves as often as possible to hide them. I finally resolved to call on my old friend Fixit to see if he could help me. Pleased at my invitation, he came willingly armed with bandages and bottles of potions. After giving him a tour of the castle we sat down in the drawing room where I told him my troubles. Delighted to give me his advice, he began to apply his remedies and compresses. Suddenly, I looked up in surprise to find my King standing in the doorway.

I quickly tried to explain, but my King silenced me with a gentle but firm glance. He led me up to our bedroom and asked me to wait there until he returned. Anticipating his reappearance in fear and trembling, my mind raced with questions. What could the King be thinking? What would he do to me? Would he throw me out of the castle for not acting like a proper queen?

It seemed like hours until he returned. When the door at last opened, he came in and sat next to me. Tenderly, lovingly, he gazed into my eyes and asked me "My precious queen, how are you enjoying living at the castle?"

What could I say? I knew I could never hide the truth from him, so I poured out my heart. I told him I did not deserve all his kindness and that I felt as if I needed to work hard to merit my place in his palace. He winced at this and quietly said, "Snow White, this is your home. You will never have to leave it."

At this, I dissolved into tears and could say no more. He whispered many precious words to me then and held me close. "I have set you free from the bondage you once lived through; however, only you can make the choice to throw away your old rags and embrace your new life. My love can heal your wounded heart as well as your misguided beliefs that you must work to gain my love or your place in my kingdom. But you must choose."

I know it must seem silly that I would want to keep my rags, but they were pieces of my old identity. I had been comfortable in them, and they were still a part of how I defined myself. Even so, I longed to be free and I wanted to feel at home in the castle with my King who loved me. So I picked up the pile of rags in the corner of my closet and put them in the dust bin. Pleased, I turned and smiled up at my King, but his expression indicated he was not satisfied.

Lovingly he said, "Bravely done, my queen, but will you be tempted to take them out of the trash after I leave?"

He knew me all too well. I had thought, however briefly, that perhaps I could go back and reclaim just one small item to remember it all by. I hung my head and said "You are right, my King."

He took my hand and said, "I know this is hard, but you are not alone. I am with you." Then he led me to the fireplace and one by one I placed my rags into the flames and watched the blaze consume them. I thought my tears and the ache in my heart would never stop, but at last, held in the embrace of my King, I felt a sweet peace flood through me. This is where I belonged.

I asked my King how I might occupy myself during the long days. He suggested we spend more time together just soaking in each other's love, and assured me that in due course he would have important work for me to do in the kingdom; but for now, I needed to learn to trust in his love.

I enjoyed spending extended time with my Beloved and began feeling more at home. I felt so much better that the next weeks flew by. One day, so full of love for my King and joy at our life together, I went through the castle singing and dancing, ending up in the kitchen where there were dishes waiting to be done. Without thinking I began to wash and dry, and put them away. After a time, I felt someone watching me and looked up to see my King standing in the doorway.

At first startled and then fearful as I realized what I was doing. Oh no! "Would he be angry that I had forgotten my place and done the dishes?" I thought in a panic. But my apprehension quickly melted away as I looked in His eyes. Laughing, he caught me up into his arms. As we strolled out into the garden, I asked him, "Why weren't you angry with me for doing the dishes?"

"Everything done in love is a joy and blessing. When done in love, although your hands may become calloused your heart will remain soft, humble and open to others. But when you work and strive only to earn a place or reward, the opposite happens." He turned me in his arms and placed my back against his chest. Pointing to the gardener he said, "Watch my servants. The ones who serve out of love serve the best."

As I looked at the joyful gardener, I began to understand. Though he labored hard making the grounds so beautiful, his cheerful countenance radiated great love and peace. And so I spent my days singing and dancing; and, on occasion, with love, joining the servants in tasks for my King.

I could go on but my lady in waiting is calling me to tea so I will close for now. I look forward to writing again. I so enjoy sharing my heart and my journey with you, precious Annabelle.

> *Never doubt how much you are loved,*
> *it is much more than you can imagine.*
> *Remember, you do not have to work for*
> *it. Find joy in this, Dear one.*
>
> *I remain affectionately yours,*
>
> *Snow White*

I laid the letter gently down on the coffee table, thoughts tumbling non-stop. Is that what I was doing? Trying to earn people's affections by working hard and doing all the right things so I would be more deserving? It occurred to me that I was spending a lot of time trying to "get it right" but my efforts never seemed enough and I certainly wasn't experiencing much joy in my life.

I thought back to the call from the church earlier that morning. They were looking for volunteers to help with the upcoming Thanksgiving outreach program... Of course I'd said yes. I always said yes. Yes for this and yes for that. Whatever anyone needed I volunteered my services. "Wasn't that a good thing?" I could hear myself echoing Snow White, yet I couldn't quite embrace the solution she'd found.

I had to work hard for everything in my life. My folks helped a lot with my college expenses, but felt I would appreciate my education more if I had to foot some of the bill. So I held jobs every summer, and after classes so I could pay my share of the tuition. No such thing as a free lunch! I paid my way.

Yet it went even deeper than just paying bills. I knew I "performed" a lot because deep down I wondered if people would really like who I was. Pleasing others had become a way of life. Would they, could they like the "real" me?

Somehow even church seemed to reinforce this. Do this and this and this and you can go to Heaven. Be the good little girl and do all the right things. Is that really what it was all about?

Oh, how I wanted the joy and peace Snow White had found in allowing herself to just receive love... Whoa Ann! What was I thinking? Snow White? Get a grip girl; you know this is just a fairy tale! Yes, I knew... but oh, how I wished her story to be true.

The next morning I found myself staring unenthusiastically at the sink full of dishes, the unmade bed, and the pile of clean laundry waiting to be folded. And behind me, I could almost hear the computer calling me to get busy job hunting. How could I spare even a minute? Then again, what had keeping up with all the chores and all the "should do's" accomplished lately? I hadn't noticed them producing any real fruit to speak of, and I hadn't felt much joy either.

So what did I have to lose? I picked up my Bible and opened it at random. My eyes fell on Jeremiah 31:1, "I have loved you with an everlasting love and with loving-kindness I have drawn you."

I felt warmth touch my heart. Could I believe in this kind of love? I'd been raised in Sunday school, and I knew all the stories, yet... this seemed so personal all of a sudden...like a kiss from Heaven meant just for me.

For a few minutes I pondered the possibilities of this kind of love; a love that I didn't have to work for or be good enough to receive. A quiet sense of peace enveloped me, and for the rest of the day I noticed that those everyday tasks seemed easier. I found myself smiling, and thinking of Snow White.

CHAPTER 4

The following day I woke up with the letters on my mind. Eager to read the next one, I rushed through breakfast and got Mark off to work. With as much efficiency as I could muster, I hurriedly cleaned up around the house, all the while anticipating what Snow White would share with me today. I didn't care that it wasn't real; at least it gave me something to look forward to. At last I sat down in my favorite chair and eagerly opened the next envelope.

Dearest Annabelle,

I hope you will forgive the brevity of this missive as it will be considerably shorter than my last. I imagine you might think that a monarch of my... shall we say, 'experience', would have hours of leisure. That may be true in some kingdoms, but in my King's realm there is never a dull moment, and today I have a busy court schedule. Therefore my darling goddaughter, I will hesitate no longer to come to the subject of this letter.

I sincerely regret that many of the day-to-day events from my early years at the castle have faded; however, this is one of the things I will never forget.

Once I became convinced that my King's love for me was not based on any work I could perform, I began to feel more confident about being his queen. For a time this new found contentment, choosing to trust and freedom from the past gave me peace, but then little by little an occasional stray doubt would arise about my stepmother.

Early on the dwarves had assured me they had "gotten rid" of her, and yet I discovered I still had some nagging fear. What if she pursued her search for me, and came back while the King was away? What if the wicked queen came disguised again and I failed to recognize her? Would she destroy the wonderful life my King had given me?

These thoughts were becoming more frequent and instead of dismissing them as I once had, I started dwelling on them. That old familiar panic set in and the joys of court life diminished. I dreaded being alone while the King was away, but I found myself too ashamed to share my fears with him, and took to hiding in our wardrobe when he left on kingdom business. I lost weight and my already fair complexion grew ashen as I spent less time in the gardens and more time in our armoire.

One day I fell asleep inside my hideaway, and that is where my King found me. I wanted to excuse myself by pretending I had been cleaning it out, but one look at his face and I knew I would not be able to hide the truth from him. Haltingly, I told him of my fears about my stepmother.

He listened patiently and finally said, "I am so glad you chose to share your fears with me. I can help with that. I have a special mirror I want to give you."

Alas, at the mere mention of the word "mirror" I shivered and turned away from him. The only "special" mirror I knew about was the treacherous one my stepmother used, and it had caused terrible trouble for me. I wanted nothing to do with any kind of magical mirror, even one given to me by my King.

He knew what was bothering me, of course; he always seemed to know, but he patiently waited for me to tell him. It took me some time to get the words out... Mercy! Even speaking about it gripped me with fear! But my wonderful King understood, and set about dispelling my worries.

He explained how the enemy enjoyed altering the good things created by my King, by making copies of them that were corrupted, as with my step-mother's mirror.

Then quietly, almost coaxingly, he said, "Snow White, if you can be brave enough to accept and use this gift, it will be another opportunity for you to learn to trust me completely."

I can recall the tenderness in his voice now, "Whenever you look into my mirror you will see me instantly and be able to perceive exactly where I am at that moment. And always, whenever you wish, you can call out to me. I will immediately come to you, so you never need to be afraid while I am away."

Even after he revealed many other wonderful uses for the mirror, I remained skeptical. Burning my rags had been difficult but looking into the mirror posed an even greater challenge!

The next day when the King went out, once again I felt those same old concerns begin to overwhelm my mind. Oh, to be free and at peace! But it seemed strange to think I could overcome my fears by doing the very thing I dreaded to do, which was to look in the mirror. But at last I lifted off the ornate cover and peered into its silvery surface. There was my Beloved! I could see him as he settled some dispute between two of his nobles. Although he never looked directly at me, I could tell he knew I used his mirror and it brought him pleasure. I watched for some time until peace fully dispelled my quaking heart. How wonderful! I could observe my King at any time and I knew if I needed him, he would come quickly riding on his powerful white steed.

I used this precious gift often after that. I enjoyed seeing where and what my King was doing, and knowing he would come to me the instant I needed him. I also began to experiment with the other marvels he had shown me about the mirror. It could reveal how the King saw me, and this helped much more than I expected. Whenever I felt as though I *deserved to be in rags or that I was unworthy of his love, the mirror would show me the truth of who I am through the eyes of my beloved King.*

Oh my dear, I must stop here as today's court session is about to begin. How I wish I had more time. Yet, even though my words here are few, I want to encourage you; do not let fear get in your way! You are loved, and love conquers all! Trust and find your fears groundless.

Lovingly, Your Godmother

Snow White

I laughed out loud imagining Snow White hiding in the closet but then sobered as I realized the message was actually hitting pretty close to home. Looking over at the mounting stack of bills on the desk, I immediately felt that old familiar dread and unrelenting pressure take hold of my heart. Nagging "what ifs" constantly played in the back of my mind.

What if Mark was laid off again? What if we lost our tiny apartment? What would we do? Where would we go? Just thinking about it made my heart race and my stomach churn. Yep, no doubt about it, I could spiral pretty quickly to that place of fear. Too bad I didn't have a magic mirror to give me confidence.

That night I lay awake and thought about Snow White's last letter. The concluding sentiments kept echoing in me, "You are loved and love conquers all. Trust and find your fears groundless." How I wanted to believe that!

As I drifted off, her words began to play melodiously through my mind. "You are loved... You are loved..." As I listened to that precious song I fell into a peaceful sleep, sweeter than any I had enjoyed for ages.

I awoke the next morning amazingly refreshed and found a new spring in my step as I got ready for the busy day ahead. I knew I didn't have a lot of time, but the devotional on my night stand beckoned me. I looked at it guiltily realizing it had been months since I'd even opened it. Snatching it up, I turned to the reading for the day: "Fear not, for I am with you; Be not dismayed, for I am your God. I will strengthen you, yes, I will help you, I will uphold you with My righteous right hand". Isaiah 41:10

I couldn't help but smile. Peace flowed over me as I let the words soak into my heart, and a new thought popped into my head. Maybe, just maybe the Scriptures were like Snow White's mirror giving me that sense of serenity. Could there be a whole lot more to those ancient words than I had ever imagined? I'd have to think about that for awhile.

When I got the mail later that morning it was filled with a new batch of overdue bills. My heart sank. I could feel the cold hand of fear begin to drag me down. In desperation I reached out to God... for the words that had given me such a sense of peace that morning. I thought, "Lord, rescue me from this whirlpool that's trying to pull me under!"

My heart raced as I opened my Bible and read again "Fear not, for I am with you...I will strengthen you....I will help you." Here was God's promise to me...to me, Ann Richards. Little by little I felt the stress drain away and hope rise up. God would help us. He could see us through. All would be okay. I didn't know how and couldn't figure it out logically, but it seemed as if God's hand was reaching into the storm of my life and somehow speaking peace to the wind and the waves of our circumstances.

As the day progressed, I held tight to those words, and whenever the panic tried to rise up I would repeat them in my heart. Unbelievably, the hours passed quickly and almost pleasantly. Instead of being lost in a cloud of worry, or preoccupied with our situation, I felt the first real glimmer of faith that God would see us through.

When Mark got home that night, I greeted him with a smile and kiss. At his quizzical look I felt a pang of regret as it dawned on me how often this past year I'd welcomed him home with sad eyes and tales of woe about which bill collectors had called and how fruitless I felt in my job search. I pulled him into a tight hug and he smiled down at me. His face relaxed and all the worry lines smoothed out into the grin I loved so much.

Dinner consisted of just a simple meal of lentil stew (my mom's favorite recipe)[1] and bread, but as we sat down to eat I let go of my misgivings about what we lacked, and felt a flood of gratefulness for what I had. There was a roof over our heads, food on the table, and most important of all, there was Mark to share it with.

For the first time in a long while we didn't talk about money or disappointments, but kept our conversation

---

1   *See Recipe on Page 172*

light and easy. We chatted amiably, at times laughing as he described how the kids who lived in the neighborhood around the house he was painting loved to clown around. As we sat talking together that night, just sharing little things, somehow our problems didn't seem so big.

Later, as I turned out my bedside lamp I found myself thinking that with God and each other we really might be able to face whatever is thrown at us. Somehow thoughts of tomorrow didn't seem so dark and hopeless.

CHAPTER 5

Before I knew it November arrived to usher in the holiday season and though I'd wanted to get back to Snow White's letters, life got in the way. I usually looked forward to all the grocery shopping and cooking for Thanksgiving which flowed directly into preparations for Christmas' arrival right on its heels. However, with all the juggling our budget required I was genuinely grateful when the invitation came to join Mark's parents for Thanksgiving dinner.

I love the holidays and enjoy making them special, but I really didn't think we'd be able to pull together everything we'd need for the normally festive feast. Usually we went to my folks' place, but they were going on a mission trip to Mexico and wouldn't be back until early December. While I cheered their willingness to help others in need, my heart missed the love and warmth of my family.

Traditionally we would arrive early, and while Mark and dad watched football, mom and I would hang out in the kitchen prepping and cooking, tasting and laughing. Once all our favorite dishes were done we'd come together around the table to share our love and enjoy the best food of the year.

Every Thanksgiving I made my favorite dish, sweet potato casserole. Not just any recipe, this invention included pineapple and coconut with a tasty, crunchy topping. It was such a family hit, Mark called it, "Ann's famous sweet potato casserole." My mouth watered just contemplating this delicious creation.[1]

Not wanting to miss out this year and thinking how my in-laws would enjoy it, I called Nelda to let her know I would bring it as our addition to the feast. "What makes it famous?" She asked.

Eagerly I shared about our long standing family tradition and how Mark had named it that because it was my very favorite dish at Thanksgiving.

I scrimped and saved over the next couple of weeks for the special ingredients I needed, and then counted down the days to the seasonal banquet.

Thanksgiving morning found us bundled up against the brisk Michigan weather to make the three hour drive to Mark's parent's home. My tummy rumbled in response to the tantalizing aroma of my special offering for today's meal. The scent of sweet cinnamon and spicy nutmeg filled the car and I could barely wait to share it with Mark's family.

As we drove, I thought back to how long it had been since we'd visited Tom and Nelda's home. Granted, we had very busy lives. Then the economic challenges hit, gas prices escalated and, with one excuse or another, we rarely made the trip. But maybe a deeper reason was because they were more reserved and formal than my folks and to me that felt less welcoming. Even after eleven years

---

1   See Recipe on Page 173

of marriage to their son, I didn't really know them all that well, and I still felt a little uncomfortable around them.

As I watched the naked trees and winter-like scenery pass by the passenger window I found myself hoping that the festiveness of the holiday might make this visit different. Trying to be optimistic, I fought down my nerves and resolutely determined to have a good time.

Arriving about an hour early for dinner, we knocked at the imposing door of my in-laws palatial home. Welcoming us in, Nelda took my treasured offering, while Tom got our coats. I followed Nelda into the kitchen asking, "What can I do to help?" But she simply shooed me away saying it was all covered, casually setting my sweet potatoes on the back counter without another word.

I joined the men in the living room just as my sister-in-law and her family came noisily through the front door. An uneasy surprise to say the least! Nelda had told me they were spending the holiday with Jack's family, but apparently an unexpected illness had changed their plans and now here they were.

Missy hadn't changed a bit over the years. As competitive as ever, her constant stream of conversation highlighted her many accomplishment. Of course she was a better cook, better wife, better dressed, you name it... she was better. Ugh!

With one glance I could see her family had grown. Two youngsters circled her and it was evident another one was on the way. Her blossoming figure touched a sore spot in me and, in growing dismay, I brushed my fingers over my tight, flat tummy. Oh, how I hoped Mark had told her I was unable to conceive! It was hard enough seeing her growing family. I couldn't handle another conversation about my defective body, especially with Mrs. Competitive.

I tried to avoid getting cornered by her, but before long she attached herself to me, talking a mile-a-minute. I tried to appear interested and listened politely as she detailed the joys of motherhood, the brilliance of her kids, and all the advantages they were receiving at the fine private school they could afford. My mind wandered and I wondered if I could get through another minute. Just when I thought I couldn't take anymore, tempting aromas would waft through the house and give me the courage to hang in there.

She continued to drone on non-stop, and I began to hope we might actually get to dinner before she paused for breath. How I wish we would've. Before I could escape she turned her keen eyes on me and I could feel an ugly sense of dread rise up and squeeze my heart.

"So when are you two going to give me some nieces or nephews to spoil? It's about time!" Even though I knew the question might come up, I wasn't prepared for it. I felt the room closing in. I couldn't breathe, much less respond. I muttered some excuse as I stood and made a beeline for the restroom, tears barely held in check.

In the privacy of the guest bath I took several deep breaths and splashed a little cool water on my face. How could Missy be so thoughtless? She must know I wanted children and it was a sore subject. Her comments were callous and cruel. I longed to escape, but like a caged beast, felt impossibly trapped. I had to go back out there.

After a few more minutes, feeling somewhat composed, I came out determined to find someone to have a "safe" discussion with. I headed for Mark and Jack hoping their conversational waters would be calmer, but as I joined them Jack turned to me and asked "How's the job hunt going?"

Oh no! Warning bells went off in my head saying, "Not safe! Not safe!" Didn't Mark's family know anything about us? Weren't they the least bit aware of our personal and financial circumstances? Honestly, my in-laws could use some sensitivity training!

Jack seemed oblivious to my lack of response or the stunned expression on my face as he launched into a showy telling of how, after having been on unemployment for less than a month, he had "fallen into" his amazing new job.

Just when I thought the hour would never end, Nelda called us in to dinner. I inwardly groaned to see my place-card right next to Missy. Great! Yet another opportunity to endure more of her endless monologue about the unsurpassed greatness of the Sorrel family, I sighed under my breath.

Once seated, we all bowed our heads for Tom to bless the food. He intoned a long, dry prayer that I thought fell short of thankfulness; then again, maybe it was the unpleasant filter over my vision.

With a mental shake, I told myself, "Lighten up a little. How bad could it be?" Everything smelled wonderful, and my flavorful addition to the meal would be a reminder of happier holidays. I quietly anticipated the delighted ohhs and ahhs of my dinner companions as they sampled my delicious delicacy.

When I opened my eyes, I hungrily searched the table for my favorite part of the feast, my sweet potato casserole. Not spotting it immediately, I scanned again. With a sinking heart I realized it wasn't there. Instead, sitting just to the left of me sat a dish overflowing with burned marshmallows and looking suspiciously like some kind of cafeteria-style candied yam mixture. What was *it* doing here? Nelda knew I was bringing sweet potatoes so why hadn't she served them rather than that overcooked mess? I knew it could be no accident and I couldn't seem to stop myself from blurting out, "Where's my sweet potato casserole?"

Without even looking up, Nelda simply replied, "Missy's kids like this kind better."

What? I felt like I'd been slapped. I thought I'd explode. I knew I'd told Nelda how important this treasured tradition was to me. It just wouldn't be Thanksgiving without it. Obviously none of that mattered to her or anyone else at the table. No one seemed to care that my feelings were hurt, or that my favorite dish had been swept aside. Platters and bowls kept passing, everyone focused on dishing up their own plates as if it was no big deal.

I kicked Mark under the table hoping he would stop chewing and speak up for me. But he ignored the plea in my eyes and gave me that "just let it go" look. I couldn't. As politely as I could manage, I asked, "Can we serve mine as well?"

Nelda looked at me coolly. "Since we didn't need it, I sent it over to the homeless shelter with Tom."

I remembered that he'd slipped out for a while shortly after we'd arrived; now I knew why.

"How could you?" I nearly shouted. "It's my special recipe." Looking at Mark I added, "My famous recipe."

Tom tried to calm me down, "Now, now. That doesn't sound very thankful or giving. Think of all those less fortunate than us who will be enjoying it."

No. Something snapped inside me. I couldn't and wouldn't imagine it. I didn't believe for one minute that they could possibly appreciate the time, care, and love I had poured into that dish. If my own family couldn't, how could a gym full of strangers? Let them eat this marshmallow mush; I wanted my casserole back! For me, it was the last straw. Broken, yet angry, I confronted my in-laws, "How could you treat me like this?"

Jack looked at me like I was insane, "What's wrong with you? Good grief, it's just a casserole! Have some of this one."

How could I explain that it wasn't just a casserole to me? It was my gift to the celebration of the day. How could I make them understand that the dish they had so easily discarded was an expression of love that I'd wanted to share with them?

Appetite gone, I pushed away from the table. I couldn't stay in their house another minute. Grabbing my coat, I fled to the car. I thought I'd freeze before Mark finally came out 20 minutes later looking miserable. Obviously angry, he slammed the car door and pulled out of the driveway in a hurry.

With a sinking heart I realized it would be a long and very chilly ride home that night. Any hopes of my gallant prince standing up for me vaporized. The rumbling in my stomach finally got Mark's attention, and without a word he pulled into a drive-in to feed me burgers and fries. I couldn't imagine a worse Thanksgiving. What a joke! Thanksgiving was absent from our house and our hearts.

CHAPTER 6

My mind continued to replay the events of that day. Over the following week I revisited every harsh word exchanged, seeing again the hurt on each face. But my own wounds were foremost in my mind. I never wanted to go to Tom and Nelda's home again, ever.

How could they be so insensitive? It wasn't about the casserole; that had just been the final blow. Everything about their disdainful attitudes in general... the thoughtless questions and comments, the competitiveness, and the cold way they seemed to view our current circumstances as if they were entirely my fault. No, I couldn't let it go, and I could never go back.

To make matters worse, Mark was barely speaking to me. Thanksgiving had been a disaster, and I understood how he could feel upset, but I'd really hoped he would at least try to see my side. Even more, I wished he would've stood up for me.

With a groan I sank down on the couch. My eyes fell on the packet of letters. Grasping for any distraction, I opened the next one in the pile hoping it might at least give me something to think about other than my wounded pride and bitter heart.

My Dear Annabelle,

This might well be one of the hardest letters I will write to you because it tells the story of one of my more challenging lessons. You might find it is difficult to read as well. But the message is an important one so I hope you find the courage to read it through to the end.

One day, during my second year as queen, while making my way down the corridor to the music room, I heard my name mentioned and paused to listen.

It was a conversation between two of our servants, and in a conspiratorial rasp the first one was saying, "...Snow White used to dress in rags and scrub the castle floors like a servant. It makes me think she is unfit to be our queen. I wonder why the King chose her instead of someone more suitable?"

The other heaved a huge sigh and replied, "Well, I heard that her step-mother ruined her. Otherwise she might have been a great queen, but now... well, I doubt that she can ever amount to much."

Then even quieter than before, the first one continued, "I think she spent too much time with those dwarves and probably picked up some of their bad habits."

Horrified at what I heard, I felt paralyzed. I wish I had left immediately and peered into my King's mirror, but my feet felt frozen where I stood. As I slowly sank to the floor I felt the coldness of the stones seep into my very heart. I wondered how many of our other servants thought the same things. For that matter, perhaps it was not limited to the inhabitants of the castle, maybe the whole kingdom was against me!

My mind reeled. Why, oh why, did my father have to marry that evil woman? Bitterness about my whole life welled up in my heart. Memories washed over me that I had not thought of for some time and I could not help but dwell on them. They were trivial at first, like petty things with the dwarves, but they soon became more serious. I once again felt resentment about my mother's death, and the deep sorrow of my father's demise. But above all, I nurtured a cold hatred for my stepmother.

It consumed me so much that I refused dinner that evening and went straight to bed fuming. I did not want to see my King, nor did I want him to see me feeling so hateful. By morning I had managed to bury much of my bitterness and thought I would be able to hide it from my husband, but my King knew me too well.

Immediately after breakfast he took me aside into his study. Looking deep into my eyes he said, "Dearest, you have done well and are nearly ready to begin preparing for the special work I have for you. However, your training cannot commence until you learn one more very important lesson."

This piqued my interest and promised a welcomed diversion from my embittered feelings. "Anything," I said. "I will do anything to be ready!"

"My dearest Snow White, so far you have learned to trust me, and you have discovered what I think of you. You have donned my garments of love, and you have overcome your fears. Soon you will be fully equipped to come with me to battle the enemies of our kingdom, but first you must defeat the battle in your heart. You must now learn to forgive. You must forgive your stepmother."

You cannot imagine the violent revolt of my heart to these words! I felt the blood drain from my face then suddenly rush back into my cheeks. As I turned and ran from the room I could hear him calling to me, "My beloved, you said you would do anything…"

It was true, I had said I would do anything; but that was before I knew what he would ask of me. How could he even think it? Surely he could never begin to understand how I felt about her. He was not the one who had been beaten and starved and subjected to slavery. She did not deserve forgiveness, and every fiber of my being cried out against the unfairness of it.

I wanted to get as far away from my King as possible, but where to go? Though I had never been there, I knew there was a basement in the castle and I searched for some time before finally finding the right passage. The steps were steeper than I had imagined, but I barely slowed at all as I hurried down them.

It astonished me how long it took to finally get to the bottom, as if the staircase descended into hell itself, and that was precisely what it felt like. I spent a day and a night in that cold, wet basement, imprisoned by my bitterness. All the while I relived every injustice, every slight, and every incident against me. No. I could never do it; there was just too much to forgive. Exhausted, I at last fell into a restless sleep and began to dream.

In the dream, I saw my King... my generous, kind, and good King in chains and being beaten! As lash after lash struck his beautiful body, I recoiled at the vivid and awful sight and awoke screaming, "NO"!

I ran up the stairs as fast as I could. I must find my King. Searching through room after room proved fruitless until I thought to look in the study where I had left him the day before. He was sitting exactly where I had left him, looking as if he had not eaten or slept and with such sadness in his eyes that I ran to him.

As I reached out for him, he took me in his arms. We just held one another for a long time. At last, he gently lifted my face up to his and said "I have something to show you."

Picking up the special mirror he had given to me, he asked me to look in it. As I did, I saw my King reflected there, weeping as he gazed at something in the distance. What was he seeing that had broken his heart? I wondered. Following his gaze, I gasped to see myself pictured there, too. This was a reflection of the past... my past. He watched me from afar as I was being beaten by my stepmother. "You were there?" I asked the King.

Tears shining in his eyes he replied, "Yes, my beloved."

"Why didn't you come rescue me then?" I demanded.

"Oh my precious queen, remember how you ran away the first time you saw me? I wanted to take you away then and there, but you were not ready and I could never force you. Had I done so I would have been no better than your stepmother. I had to wait in agony and love until the right time."

At that moment I remembered my dream and asked him, "Was my dream true? Were you also beaten and chained?"

"Yes, my treasure. I know what you went through because many years ago I experienced it too. I had to forgive those who mistreated me just as I had to forgive your stepmother for what she did to you."

Almost more than I could take in, I sat silently for some time. Finally I confessed, "In truth, I do not feel like I want to, nor do I know how, but if you will help me I am willing to forgive her."

As he held me close, I felt his pleasure with me, and heard his assurance that it was his delight to help me. It took time, patience, and love, but gradually my feelings followed my commitment to forgive.

It was not an easy lesson, my dear. Forgiving is hard work. But oh, I felt so much better once I did it. I know your life will be filled with many opportunities to offer forgiveness and, for your sake, I pray that you will learn to forgive quickly. The freedom you receive in return is well worth the effort. Start by making the commitment to forgive, whether you feel like it or not... Your feelings will follow in time.

Lovingly yours,

Snow White

Wow... what a difficult letter! And the timing! I had a hard time finishing it as it hit so close to home. Several times I'd set it down, but the desire to see how it ended and Snow's dare to find courage kept me picking it back up. Her words had given me so much to process.

In all honesty, stewing about the Thanksgiving fiasco over the last couple of days hadn't been any fun. I knew I needed to take responsibility for my own actions and reactions. While I couldn't change how Mark's family acted, I could definitely alter how I responded. As hard as it was going to be, I would have to find a way to let go of my offended and hurt feelings, and try and make peace with my in-laws. I hoped Snow was right about my feelings following my choice to forgive, because I certainly didn't feel like it right now.

Above everything else, I needed to patch things up with Mark. Maybe he would enjoy a special dinner tonight. Hmmm...I could make his favorite grilled steak with mushrooms – seasoned generously with a helping of heartfelt apology for my part in the whole mess.[1] Yes, a good "peace" offering was definitely better than a sour wife. My heart was already feeling lighter than it had in a long time.

The day flew by as I shopped for just the right ingredients and then carefully prepared them the way Mark preferred. As the time drew near for his arrival, I took a quick shower, changed into my best dress and waited. Wistfully glancing at the table, I wished I had some fresh flowers for a centerpiece, but I'd splurged enough on dinner and would have to be especially careful if we wanted to eat the rest of the month.

Hearing Mark's car in the driveway, I brushed that gloomy thought away. Putting on what I hoped was a cheerful face, I ran to the window. My heart dropped as I saw his face hardened into a grimace as he approached the house. This was going to be harder than I thought.

For a moment my resolve fluttered. Would this work? Was reconciliation possible? I put on the brightest smile I could muster and threw open the door.

---

1   *See Recipe on Page 174*

Oh, if only you could have seen Mark's face! From frown to surprise to delight in less than 10 seconds. He opened his arms to me and I fell gladly into his embrace.

I will leave the rest of the evening to your imagination, only to say that humble pie may be difficult at first, but the fruit of forgiveness is truly sweet.

I knew I had more I would need to do, including writing some letters of my own, but for now this was a step in the right direction.

CHAPTER 7

Christmas arrived with the usual hustle and bustle of sending cards, endless shopping, and of course, Christmas parties. The holiday crowds were as hurried and harried as ever, traffic snarled near every shopping center and our finances were still tight with no relief in sight. Yet a sense of contentment filled me, carrying me through it all. Even the church's Christmas Eve service seemed more meaningful this year.

Mark had noticed I'd been smiling more and one evening he asked me quizzically, "Who are you, and what have you done with my wife?" Then more seriously, "Really, Hon, you seem...lighter, more at ease."

Surprised by his question, it dawned on me he was right. Change was happening inside me, though how could I explain it? Could it be because of my Aunt Annabelle's letters? How could I tell him a fairy tale was transforming my life?

As I mentally debated whether to share the source of my metamorphosis, he stood there looking at me with that little grin tugging at the corner of his lips that I loved. How could I resist? As silly as it all sounded, I told him everything, describing the letters I had read so far and the wisdom I'd gained.

I braced myself, fully expecting Mark to laugh at the notion that a fairy tale character could be having such an impact on my life. Instead, he took my hand in his and tenderly said, "I like how they're changing you. When are you planning to read the next one?" His smile broadened as he gently brushed a soft kiss over my knuckles and left me sitting on the sofa. Not the reaction I had expected!

After the conviction I'd felt from my last inheritance letter, I was a little bit reluctant to read any more. My mind and heart were still working overtime with the whole forgiveness issue. Who knew how this next one might hit me? That said, I knew the time had come, so while Mark busied himself on the computer, I sat down by the fireplace to warm myself in its comforting glow and slowly opened the envelope.

Dearest Annabelle,

I trust you will enjoy this missive much more than my last. I am afraid I will need to keep this short as my appointment book is full today, but I wanted to get off a few lines to you about the next chapter of my story.

The day at last came when my King requested that I don my very best gown and meet him in the castle's chapel to participate in a very special ceremony. Arriving, I discovered the room filled with nobles and ladies of the court. As I entered, my King beckoned me to the front of the sanctuary and at his request I knelt before him.

"I have called and chosen you to be my queen, to serve our people, and to defend this kingdom. The time has now come for you to become my warrior queen, and to join me on the battlefield, fierce and loyal, brave and true, my faithful companion. At my side you will face many difficulties and challenges, but the rewards will make them all worthwhile. Together, we will protect our kingdom from the enemy's attacks. We will expand and enlarge our borders. This day I commission you, my Warrior Queen."

Humbled by this, I bowed my head as he took his sword in hand and tapped the top of each of my shoulders with the blade. As he bid me arise and face the court he announced to all, "Behold, my Warrior Queen."

My heart felt overwhelmed with joy and awe at his declaration. Imagine my surprise when he then placed a camouflage cloak over my beautiful white robes, and handed me a pair of hobnailed boots to wear! I did my best to smile graciously, but the coat and boots appeared so ugly, I wondered briefly what the castle staff would say about this.

With the ceremony complete, the court was dismissed, and my King directed me to his study where we could talk privately. As soon as the door closed, I asked him, "Why do I have to wear this unattractive cloak over my beautiful white robes?"

At his silence, I became fearful he might feel hurt by my question, so I hurried to continue. "It is just that I cannot imagine they complement each other. Perhaps I should wear something different underneath; something more appropriate? Wearing these together just seems so... incongruent."

Chuckling he responded, "I know what you are thinking, my beloved. You believe that maybe your old work clothes would be a better match for the camouflage coat and heavy boots." He paused and then continued more seriously. "But your regal robes are an indispensable part of your combat wardrobe. The camouflage is essential to hide you from the enemy and allow you to launch secret attacks without being seen. Your queenly robes underneath are the mark of my authority on you to do battle, and they will dazzle and stun the enemy at close range. You would have some protection if you chose to fight with this camouflage over rags, but in the heat of battle the enemy would notice that you were fighting without my mark of authority, and it would give him an advantage to harm you."

Quite obviously I had much to learn about warfare and maybe some things to unlearn! In addition to the right attire, my King gave me a sword of my own, a shield, and other important implements of armor.

In the days that followed he taught me how to correctly use each piece of my new weaponry. Some were for offensive warfare, and others were for defense, and I soon learned the importance of each.

My first actual confrontation with the enemy both frightened and excited me. I expect it seemed a mere skirmish to the seasoned troops, but to this novice it was quite an adventure.

The battle ebbed-and-flowed as each side attacked, defended, advanced and retreated; and through it all I was in the thick of it. Waving my sword around a great deal, dodging arrows, I then joined the charge that put the enemy to flight.

On the way home the excitement faded some and I began to think that my part in the fight had not really been all that much help. I found myself hoping I would be able to accomplish more for the kingdom next time.

That night in our bedchamber my King encouraged me to look into his special mirror. When I peered into it I could see the battle replayed exactly as it had happened, yet at the same time somehow different than I remembered. As I watched, I saw a dazzling light flash from my white robes that terrified and scattered the enemy before us.

The power of the light amazed me and I was flooded with joy at the realization that my part really had made a difference to the outcome of the battle. That joy was followed closely by profound thankfulness to my King, for I knew without his robes, without the preparation he had given me, and most of all, without his power and presence there with me I could not have accomplished so much.

That was many years ago, and since then I have fought in more battles than I can recount. Some were small and brief, while others were major and lasted for weeks or months at a time.

As I look back over the years, I can see that mistakes were made... sometimes by me, sometimes by others. But regardless of who made them, these blunders would inevitably lead to one of us being wounded, or to giving the enemy a chance to gain precious ground. At first I was devastated by these setbacks, but my King assured me that if I would steadfastly trust him, everything would eventually work to our advantage before the end. As always, he was right.

My lady in waiting is summoning me to my next appointment and so I must close for now, but I hope you have been encouraged today. But before I seal this letter allow me to leave you with these truths: Battles will come, my dear. You will make mistakes. There will be wounds. But always remember, in the hand of the King all things work out for your best good.

Tenderly yours,

Snow White

At the thought of Snow White dressed in camouflage and combat boots, I giggled out loud. Glancing up from the page, I discovered both Mark and our cat Simon, looking at me to determine what I found so amusing. "Read it to me, Ann," Mark entreated. "I could use a good laugh."

As I read this latest letter to them, I knew Mark was enjoying it as much as I had. He laughed in all the right places and nodded his agreement with the wisdom of the King. On the other hand, Simon merely watched us coolly with his intelligent green eyes, then yawned as if to say "So what's the big deal anyway?"

All in all, it was a wonderful evening. I loved being able to share the letters with Mark and wondered why I had kept them to myself for so long. Even though my "inheritance" hadn't brought us financial gain, somehow it was drawing us closer and I could see great value in that. I felt different and though the changes were subtle, I liked them. My life seemed better, brighter.

Lying in bed that night, Snow's closing words continued to spin in my mind, "You will make mistakes. There will be wounds. But always remember, in the hand of the King all things work out for your best good."

Was it really true? How could making a mess of things turn out to be for my "best good?" For a long time now I'd been spending nearly every waking moment trying to avoid mistakes and do everything "right", but it seemed that the harder I tried, the more I failed. And with those failures came wounds.

As I lay sleepless next to my softly snoring husband, I felt a prayer bubble right up from my heart, "Jesus, I want to give You all my messes and mistakes. Will You take them and make things right?" As the words left my mouth I felt my chest unclench and my heart soften.

Wow. Until that very moment I'd rarely prayed spontaneously, so that impulsive little prayer startled me. My previous prayer life had largely been limited to the formal prayers I'd learned at church. But this felt so... so good, so natural and intimate, hardly like praying at all... more like I was just talking to the Lord as I would a friend.

Suddenly the card I'd received in the mail today from Nelda came to mind. A Hallmark card and very sweet, but even nicer was her personal note. She thanked me for my recent letter to her, and then asked my forgiveness for her thoughtlessness in giving away my casserole.

As I lay there mentally thanking her for the nice gesture it hit me... The Lord was already answering my prayer to heal the rift between my mother-in-law and me! Immediately, thankfulness washed over me for everything He was doing in my life...for redeeming my mistakes, for mending my messes, and for working things out for my "best good."

CHAPTER 8

How could five letters make such a difference? I thought one afternoon several months later. Revealing them to Mark had at first been difficult, but now I enjoyed the camaraderie of having someone to share them with.

It got me thinking about the history of these letters. How far back did they go? How many generations of my family had been recipients of them? What were their stories? With Aunt Annabelle gone, the only one who might know anything was my mom.

When I'd first picked up the chest those many months ago, she had called shortly after inquiring after my inheritance. I'd been vague at the time, not yet convinced of the value of the manuscripts and far from being ready to share anything. But now the time had come for questions to be answered, mine and hers.

After consulting Mark and our budget, we agreed on a surprise trip to my parents. Putting new tires on my Volkswagen and an oil change would stretch us, but couldn't be put off in light of the five hour drive to Gainesville.

Initially, Mark planned to come with me and we'd eagerly anticipated the trip since vacations were few and far between. However, the day before we were to leave, Mark was offered a large painting job that couldn't be turned down. Disappointed, but believing there was purpose in it, I left the next morning alone.

Getting away from the confines of our apartment felt amazing and I relished the freedom of the road. As mile after mile glided by, I reminisced about my previous journey to that dingy attic many months ago. Remembering the anticipation and excitement I'd felt on the way and the letdown of the return trip. I could laugh now at the tumultuous emotions of that time and marvel at God's good grace through the journey thus far.

Before I knew it, I stood before my parent's door, wondering just how this would play out. At my knock, my mom, slowly cracked open the door, then in surprise, threw it wide, immediately embracing me in her ample arms. Before I could take a breath, she turned, calling out "Annabelle's home!" to my father before nearly smothering me again with hugs. It felt funny to hear her call me "Annabelle" after reading the letters. How annoyed I'd been in the past that she was the only one who insisted on calling me that. Yet somehow now I didn't mind so much.

"Well, to what do we owe the privilege of this visit?" my dad inquired as he kissed me on the cheek.

"Just look at her! She's glowing! Is it....?" My mom asked hopefully.

For a moment, a pang went through me as I realized what she was thinking, but I didn't want to ruin the joy of the day with those thoughts so quickly interjected, "No Mom, just some...uh...things I wanted to talk to you about."

"Well, how grand! You look just marvelous! Can't wait to hear all about it," she gushed while ushering me in and at the same time ordering, "Henry, get her things from the car!"

I was home! Fingering the old sofa, memories of my childhood fast forwarded through my mind. My mom sat across from me, ready to get down to business, peppering me with questions, but I felt suddenly shy regarding the reason I'd come.

My dad seemed to understand as he walked back in the door carrying my suitcase. Setting it down in the hallway, he reached for my mom, laying a hand on her shoulder he said, "Margaret, let her catch her breath! She didn't come for an interrogation. She'll tell us when she's ready."

I smiled gratefully up at him, as my mom harrumphed, "This does beat all. I will have to change my bridge game for tonight. How long are you staying?" Getting up she moved to the kitchen, calling back "Want some tea?"

Dad winked at me. "She's thrilled you're here. She really didn't want to host that bridge game anyway."

The evening flowed as my mom talked a mile a minute about this person and that, some from my childhood, other's I didn't know but she seemed to think I should. Occasionally, my dad would interject a comment or ask after Mark. Earlier than I expected, he got up and excused himself saying, "Must head to bed and let you two ladies continue," shuffling down the hallway to their room. I wasn't sure if he was just worn out or thought maybe I wanted to speak privately to mother. It wasn't that I minded sharing with him, but a part of me still hesitated.

As soon as the bedroom door closed, Mom brought the talk back around to me. "Now I must know what this trip is about, Annabelle. Is this about your inheritance?"

"Yes. I have many questions I hope you might be able to answer." I replied, then paused, trying to formulate where to start. Giving up, the questions just spilled out. "Why did you name me after Aunt Annabelle? Why did she give me the inheritance when I hardly knew her? Did she tell you about the letters? How far back have they gone?"

"Whoa, Dearie! One at a time." Now it was her turn to reflect. "Well, you know some of the story. Your brothers were 14 and 16 when we found out we were expecting you. Believe me, the surprise of our lives, but a great one, once we got used to it. My Aunt Annabelle had recently gone through some kind of transformation in her life. It was strange how she came to us one day and insisted we name you "Annabelle" after her, explaining that if we did, you would receive an inheritance since she was unmarried and had no children. It was an unusual request and an unusual name. We debated for some time, but then agreed it couldn't hurt. We grew to love the name, Annabelle. Claiming that the inheritance she had to give was worth far more than any amount of money, she hinted here and there about strange things I couldn't fully understand."

Pausing a moment for a breath, she suddenly exclaimed, "Oh my, I forgot all about the package!" She jumped up and began to pace.

Now it was my turn for excitement. "What package? Where is it?"

A few more paces before she stopped and declared, "I believe it must be in the attic. Too bad, it's too late to get to it now. We'll have to wait for morning."

She sat down thoughtfully again. "It was shortly after you were born and Annabelle came for a visit to see her namesake. She gave me a package but made me swear I wouldn't open it until she had passed on and you had gotten this mysterious "inheritance." You know me, it was one of the hardest things to not even take a peek, my curiosity so high, but I loved my aunt and wanted to honor her request. I think your dad put it away deep in the attic so I wouldn't be tempted."

Turning back to me, her keen eyes burrowing deep into mine, she said, "Now it's my turn to ask the questions. Tell me about this inheritance. I'm dying to hear all about it."

Slowly at first, but gaining confidence, I shared with her the journey of the first five letters. Watching the emotional dance on her face from surprise to shock, laughter to tears and everything in between was worth it all. She giggled at the silly dwarves, teared up at the dungeon of bitterness, and cheered Snow on as warrior queen. When I finished she asked, "Is that all? Are there more letters?"

"Yes," I replied, "I'm taking my time with each one."

"Oh, I couldn't have done that! I'd have read them all in one sitting. But maybe that's why she didn't give them to me."

After a pause, I asked, "Tell me more about Aunt Annabelle. You said she had a transformation? What was her life like?"

"Well, that is quite the story, my dear, and I'm not sure we can get to it all tonight. A strange one, mostly a loner, she never married, keeping to herself. My mother said her sister, Annabelle, had an accident when young and never fully recovered. Depression haunted her and few people could understand or reach her.

"Then, as I said, shortly before you were born something happened. Each family member had their own idea of what brought the change - everything from whispered rumors of a secret romance to a new medication or a mysterious inheritance. Whatever the reason, we were grateful to have her back at family reunions and events and such. Though she didn't reveal much about herself, her now cheerful demeanor was pleasant enough and we enjoyed her company as time allowed. As I said, though startled by her unusual request to name you after her, the enigma of it all intrigued us. We'd been told after the boys that I couldn't have any more children, both for my health and the baby's. After so many years to become pregnant, to weather the pregnancy with little complications, especially at my age, and then for you to be the girl we'd longed for seemed quite miraculous. Somehow it seemed fitting to fulfill her request. She especially adored you and loved holding you as a baby and then watching you at successive family reunions grow into such a lovely young woman." Lost in memories, my mom's last words drifted into silence.

Both of us started when the Grandfather Clock in the hall chimed midnight. I'd no idea it was this late. Kissing my mom on the cheek, I wordlessly headed down to my room. It had been a full day with many revelations, giving us both much to ponder.

As I slid under the covers of my childhood bed, I wondered if I could sleep. I wished I had known more about my Aunt Annabelle, that I could talk with her one more time and ask her the many questions on my heart. Maybe this package would reveal some of the secrets hidden away. I could hardly wait for morning light.

.

CHAPTER 9

I woke to the smell of frying bacon, sausage and eggs. Yes, I was home. Pleasant memories revolved in my head as I quickly slipped on some sweats and headed down for breakfast.

"How'd you get up so early, Honey?" My dad called out when he saw me.

"Dad, it's almost 8:30. Not so early." I replied, though relishing this fall back to childhood, this daily exchange.

"Now sit down here and have some grub. You look like you could put some meat on those bones," my mom chided.

Submitting meekly, I took my place and reached out as we held hands for the blessing. Such small gestures, yet so meaningful.

"I hear we have an attic project first thing this morning," my dad commented, to the eager assent of both my mother and I. In my excitement, I could have forgone breakfast, but knew she would never allow it, fearing I would dry up and blow away before lunch if I didn't partake of her hearty meal.

While breakfast was delicious and even more so since I didn't have to prepare it, I was anxious to get to the mystery in the attic. Mentally urging my parents to hurry as they methodically ate, then cleared the dishes, washing up and putting everything away, all the while refusing my offers of assistance. Sensing my mood, my dad said, "Patience, Ann, that package isn't going anywhere."

It seemed to take forever for my dad to get the ladder, position it correctly, open the trap door and climb up into the attic. He insisted it was no place for a lady or I would have been the first one up there. "It wouldn't do any good anyway," he postulated, "You don't know what it looks like. I do." With that, he disappeared into the dark recesses of the attic. For a long time, we heard the scrape and slide as he moved boxes and odds and ends, my mom and I waiting impatiently. Then there was an extended pause and in unison we called up eagerly, "Did you find it?"

"Just looking at my old golf clubs. Maybe I should take up golfing again."

"Dad!" I nearly yelled, heading up the ladder.

Laughing, he called "Whoa, there....just kidding. Yes...yes, I think I've found it."

Relieved, I backed down the ladder as my mom reached for the bundle.

Gathering back in the living room, my mom started to open the peculiar package. "Isn't it Ann's?" My dad queried, "She should open it."

Reluctantly, my mom handed it to me. The large overstuffed padded envelope trembled in my hand. Carefully opening the flap, out slid several old journals, a yellow notepad and a plastic container encasing what looked to be ancient parchment written in a language I could not comprehend.

Pressing closer to see, my mom exclaimed "Those should be in a museum!"

"Yes, but who would believe their authenticity? Besides, ever heard of a fairy tale museum?" he teased.

Mom attempted to jab him with her elbow, but familiar with this game, he easily moved aside, only increasing her irritation.

I turned to the yellow pad where I recognized my great aunt's spidery script.

Dearest Annabelle,

By now, hopefully, you have discovered your inheritance and, while it seems a stretch, I hope you will press into the mystery of a transformed life. Generations ago, an ancestor translated and copied the set found in the chest. Not willing to risk these precious papers, the originals were kept separate in case one was lost, the other would remain. They are yours, my darling. I trust them to your care.

Whether you decide to share with others (if they will believe you) or to keep them to yourself, as I did, is your choice. Because my mental state had been questioned by many in my family, I knew if I spoke too much of these letters, it would only confirm their suspicions of my unstable condition. I feared being committed against my will, so I chose silence.

This journey is for those desperate enough for change. Believe or disbelieve, the "proof is in the pudding" as they say, or in the fruit of a reformed life. So what if it is a forgery? Oh, the sweetness of new life! Though once mired down in pain and suffering now I walk in the light of day. I believe the same for you. Though our circumstances may vary greatly, we all battle the same demons and find our release from the same source. I trust you will find each letter meets you just in time, even when you don't think so. The arrows of truth will hit their mark if you are willing and open.

I will briefly relate my experience and your mom may be able to fill in the rest. Other's stories are recorded in the enclosed journals. Feel free to add yours when you pass it on.

At age nine, a childhood bully pushed me out of a treehouse. Landing on my right arm, shattering it in many places, I suffered greatly. With little money for a doctor, my parents did the best they could to set it, but it remained significantly disfigured and largely useless. Missing months of school, I fell further and further behind. My outward body came to mirror the inner brokenness I felt through my teens and adult years. Depression clouded my mind and at times thoughts of suicide filled me. Though I tried a few times, I lacked the courage to follow through. I might have remained always in this miserable existence if it had not been for "fate" which brought me the letters.

After my mother's funeral, I discovered a trunk in her attic. I'd loaded it into my car to take to Goodwill, but the tag caught my attention - addressed to "Anna-belle"-- and on a whim, I put it back. Sadly, it would be years later before I discovered the secret compartment and the letters, and yet they came just in time.

Collecting dust year after year in my attic, the chest's secret remained hidden, until one day I climbed the stairs, rope in hand, determined to end my misery. Moving the chest under a beam, I prepared the noose, finally determined to bring to a close my days. As I stepped onto the trunk, for some reason it flipped upside down and opened, revealing a key and the lining partially lifted up exposing the secret compartment. That moment my life changed. If you've read the letters, you understand. Though not instant, the gradual shift in perspective, the discovery of love and forgiveness, set me free to finally be who I was meant to be. I could grieve for lost years, yet I choose to rejoice in the days that are left to me and hope to leave a legacy for you, my dear.

Months after finding the letters, I wondered if there was more and began an extensive search of my mother's belongings, some of which remained in my attic. When nothing turned up, I turned to my sister (your grandmother). We sifted through many boxes, not even sure what we were looking for, but somehow the conviction grew that we would find something extra. Mildred, ready to concede defeat (or maybe thinking I was truly crazy), left me alone that final day in the attic.

With only a few boxes left to go through, I sent up a quick prayer for guidance (a new thing for me). Instead of taking the box nearest me I reached back to a large barrel we had looked in the previous day. My withered arm was of little use as I attempted to open it and I nearly gave up in frustration. I cried out again to the Lord and heard a little popping sound as the lid gave way. Buried near the bottom, I found what I was looking for, the package you now hold in your hands.

Cherish every day as a gift from God. Life is truly worth living when it is for Him and not the superficial values of this fallen world. Choose joy and hope. And you will overcome.

All my love,
Aunt Annabelle

Neither my mom nor I had a dry eye as I finished reading aloud my great aunt's story. After some moments of quiet introspection, mom groaned, "If only I'd known what she was going through....maybe..."

Dad wrapped his arms around her to comfort her. I went in search of some tissues. "How little we understand what others face when we are so absorbed in our own issues," I thought. Who around me was I blind to?

I placed the journals and the originals back into the package. We'd had enough for one day. Mark and I had agreed since I had come alone, that I could stay as long as needed. There was no rush.

We gradually dispersed to various parts of the house, each thoughtfully considering our own lives and those we loved. Lunch was a quiet affair and afterwards I went for a walk in the local park. Sitting on a swing, gently pushing myself back and forth, I relished the wind blowing against my cheeks and feeling alive. I could almost hear my aunt saying, "Precious one, live well, live whole and find love."

Arriving back at the house hours later, I smelled fresh baked cookies. There was my mom and her solution to most situations. "Come, Dearie, have a cookie and some milk and you will feel better," she called out.

Although I felt refreshed after my walk and knew it wasn't the answer, I enjoyed the feeling again of sitting in the fragrant kitchen enjoying my mom's comfort food and conversation. It was good to be home.

I retired early that night wanting to take a look at the journals in the privacy of my room. The first one dated back to 1867, the words in places smudged and the flowing script difficult to decipher. I got caught up in the story-line, tracing the trunk's journey on a covered wagon from Virginia to North Dakota, surviving Indian attacks, illness and danger. Hearing how these simple letters inspired a pioneer through great difficulties amazed me. Reaching for the next journal, I heard the clock strike two. Astonished at how fast the time had flown, I put the journal back and drew the covers up close. It would have to wait.

CHAPTER 10

Two more days of visiting and reading the journals and I felt restless. I'd gotten what I'd come for and was ready to head home. My parents would have kept me indefinitely, but I missed Mark and was anxious to get back and show him the journals. We'd talked over the phone each night, but it wasn't the same.

Getting a good night sleep, I packed quickly ready to slip out the door at the first light of day. "Oh no you don't, young lady!" my mom exclaimed, seeing me in the hallway suitcase in hand. "You sit down and eat a proper breakfast. No one leaves this house hungry."

I sighed, but complied, knowing arguing wouldn't change her mind. Sitting down to another full breakfast of omelets, hashbrowns and even French toast I figured the upside was I wouldn't be hungry again 'til dinner.

After many hugs, kisses and tears, I was on the road home. This time my mind wandered through the stories I'd read in the last couple of days. Pioneers, Pilgrims and pirates with enough adventure to fill more than one book.

I thought about how the chest came across the ocean, smuggled on board by a sailor who'd made a promise to his mother to deliver it to his second cousin in America named Annabelle. Braving pirate attacks and storms, their ship arrived battered but intact. Going from settlement to settlement, this sailor finally found Annabelle on her deathbed, ravaged by small pox. Her faithful husband read to her the letters, giving her hope in her final hours. Though disbelieving himself, in honor of his wife, he named her surviving newborn daughter, Annabelle, promising to pass on the letters to her at the appropriate time.

The chronology of the letters was incomplete. Gaps here and there existed, shrouding in mystery the where and when and how. It is possible not all of the recipients were my actual ancestors, yet I liked to believe they were, at least in spirit.

One of my favorites was a cryptic notation without even a date. This Annabelle, a nursemaid in the royal French court, covertly learned to read and write with her charges until she could at last read the documents passed down to her from her father's Aunt.

Before I knew it, I was home again in Mark's arms. We had an incredible evening catching up. Mark's analytical mind wanted to trace the letters' journey, lining up all the dates and filling in as much as possible the details that we did know. Taping together many sheets of paper, we began to painstakingly build a timeline. Because some of the notes had no dates, we stuck them in where it seemed to fill a corresponding time gap. Though not solving all the riddles or breaches, it did give a clearer picture of the saga of the letters.

By the next Saturday I felt inexplicably drawn back to my inheritance. Usually Mark and I enjoy sleeping in on the weekend, relishing the extra snooze time; but not this week. Simon woke us up bright and early yowling for attention. We tumbled out of bed to meet the day a full two hours earlier than normal. Once appeasing our demanding feline, we ate breakfast, and did the washing up together.

With no specific plans for the day, I had plenty of time to lazily enjoy a steaming mug of my favorite tea. Sitting down in the rocker by the sun dappled window, I reached for the next envelope wondering what it might contain.

Dearest Annabelle,

By now you are probably wondering about my seven dwarves. It fills me with merriment to call them that, for if you were to tell them I referred to them in this manner, they would quickly correct you by saying, "You are mistaken. She is our Snow White!"

They are dearer to me now than ever before. We have been through a great deal together, and their transformations were every bit as marvelous as my own. While I cannot go into as much detail about their changes as I have with my own, I will do my best to share the finer points.

Do you remember me telling you about the day I called Fixit to the castle to tend my rough, scratched hands? If so, then you will also recall that the King came home during that visit and escorted me from the drawing room up to our bedchamber with instructions to stay there and await his return. He went back to the drawing room to have a talk with Fixit. No, he was not upset with my diminutive friend, rather he was offering him a new way to help people that could alleviate their problems rather than merely treating the symptoms or covering them over with bandages.

As you might imagine, it took some convincing as Fixit was quite set in his ways, but the King persuaded him and soon Fixit returned regularly to the castle learning the true ways of the healer. Under the King's guidance, not only did he become skilled at applying the varied oils, ointments and poultices provided him, he also learned to see his patients as people, not just problems to be solved. Fixit eventually became known as one of the greatest healers in the kingdom, regaled for his wisdom and caring.

That was just the beginning. In the fullness of time my King touched all the dwarves' live through his caring and generosity. During one of his visits to their cottage, he asked them how long it had been since they had found a new cache of jewels or metals in their mines. Merry, full of glee and excitement was quick to tell him all about the large vein of gold discovered by his great, great, great grandfather. He, like all of his family, loved to recount stories of the days when treasure abounded. Merry would have talked on for hours had not Grumbly grown irritated by his long rendition of history and interrupted by saying "In other words, we have never found anything of value ourselves."

At this revelation the King asked their permission to visit the mines. They were delighted by his interest in their work. Gladly the dwarves showed him the lay of the shafts, and painstakingly explained all the processes and procedures of mining. The King questioned them closely on many points, and at long last asked them something that set them all to dancing... even Grumbly. His question was simple. "Would you like to find real treasure in the mines?" he asked.

Without a moment's hesitation they unanimously cheered, "Yes Sire, thank you Sire!" thinking the King must be talking about some new secret tunnel.

But instead the King surprised them by unveiling an amazing lantern of his own design. "Use this, my mighty men, exclusively for lighting your work sites, even the caverns you have abandoned as worthless, where you have found nothing."

Now you may not know this about them, but dwarves are often wary of new ideas, and even though this one came from the King, their skepticism ran deep. It didn't make sense that a new lantern would produce treasure in areas they'd been working in for years. But not wishing to seem ungrateful, they took up the lamp and proceeded into one of the tunnels.

Cries of delight and astonishment rang out as the lamp revealed emeralds, rubies, and diamonds embedded between veins of gold and silver all sparkling in blinding array! They had spent years digging in this very tunnel without success, but it took the illumination of the King's light to show them the vast treasure hidden there in the darkness. They could hardly believe their eyes.

Eager now to listen to his ideas, the dwarves paid close attention to the King's next recommendation that changed their lives every bit as much as finding the treasure. He observed that with the help of the new lantern there would no longer be a need for all of them to continue doing the very same job, "My dear dwarves, you are all fine miners, but each of you is also uniquely gifted with singular talents that you might desire to develop. If you so choose, you could use your special gifts to do much good throughout my realm."

Work outside of the mine? The very idea seemed impossible. For as long as any of them could remember they had always worked together, each doing exactly what the other six did. Being so foreign a concept to them, it took some time to implement.

Merry, Sneezer and Dimwit were thrilled to finally be excavating the jewels and precious metals they had toiled so many years for and therefore chose to continue working the mines. Fixit, Grumbly, and Snoozy still enjoyed browsing through the dwarves' new treasures, but they happily embraced the freedom they had been given to follow their hearts along new paths. My sweet, shy Timmy continued to work in the mines for a time, but eventually found his treasure in a very different place.

Once he understood that he was no longer needed at the mine, Grumbly could often be found in the company of my King. As they spent extended time together his bitterness at being shunned and continually called cursed began to heal.

The King immediately recognized Grumbly as having the rare ability to actually see things before they happened. Patiently the King helped him understand that with vision comes great responsibility. He taught him how to use this precious gift in a way that would help those around him rather than frighten them. As Grumbly learned to share these insights in an un-alarming way, people began to listen to him and heed his warnings.

I wish I had time to tell you about the great Battle of the Seven Hills. If not for Grumbly's foresight into the activity of the enemy, we would all have been ambushed and the kingdom would have suffered grave losses.

Serving the King filled my grumpy friend with great purpose and joy, and his esteem among the villagers rose. Although he never lost his forthright manner of speech, his heart became so soft and gentle that many of the young ones refused to call him by his name, and chose instead to refer to him as G-papa.

Though some transformations took longer than others, through the faithfulness of the King, not one of my little friends remained unchanged. For a long season it appeared Snoozy would live his entire life in a haze of exhausted indifference. After many years of fruitless pep talks, failed experiments, and endless poking and prodding, Snoozy at last became Fixit's first great success story.

After failing time and again Fixit finally went to the King and asked for his help. Working together, they developed a very special tonic which Snoozy took at regular intervals. Though not an immediate cure, we did begin to notice gradual changes. After several doses of the new medicine, Snoozy found himself able to stay awake for an hour or two without drifting off. As the treatments continued, his alertness steadily increased until at last he stayed awake for an entire day.

More importantly, once fully awake, he began to hunger for all the experiences he had missed in his life. Over and over, he exclaimed he felt he had slept half his life away (which was quite true), and now he wanted to make up for lost time and live every moment to the fullest. He took up a variety of daring endeavors...mountain climbing, cliff diving, boar hunting, and even jousting! Now a mighty blaze burned inside him to redeem the squandered years.

Snoozy began sharing his "new life" experience with other sleepy people and giving stirring speeches on waking up and living life to the fullest. He shared the miraculous stimulating elixir Fixit had given him with others and called many out of deathlike weariness into full and fruitful lives.

Seeing Snoozy's cure inspired Sneezer to seek healing for his allergies. Once again the King and Fixit joined forces preparing a treatment to completely alleviate Sneezer's highly unpleasant, explosive expulsions of air and mucus. Almost immediately Sneezer lost all his aforementioned irritableness. Beginning to feel so much better, he was less offended and more forgiving toward everyone around him. Even those who had once been drenched by the spray of his sneezes began to converse with him again. That of course led to his becoming aware of how many he had injured by the harsh judgments and cruel words he had once used so fluently.

Poor Sneezer regretted all the hurtfulness that had occurred because of him. Even more than just breathing without sneezing, he desired peace and companionship. He sought private counsel with the King and from that day forward Sneezer went to each and every person he had ever injured to make amends. Furthermore, when it became known that he no longer showered anyone with sneezes or unkind words, he made many friends, becoming well-loved and trusted.

Oh, my, this letter has grown long and now my maid is calling me to supper. I hate to leave you hanging, but must continue my narrative of the dwarves for another time.

Know this, Beloved Annabelle, nothing is impossible with the love of the King. The hardest character flaw, the most glaring fault can all be cured. Don't write anyone off. Love changes things.

Lovingly,

Snow White

Tempted to read the next letter to finish the dwarves' story, I reached for the next one. But something stopped me. Somehow I knew, like a good meal, the letters were meant to be pondered, digested, and incorporated into life. I would wait for the right time. Although I wondered about Merry, Dimwit and Timmy, I remembered what Aunt Annabelle had written about the letters coming at the exact moment they were needed and I obeyed the inner prompting to wait.

My thoughts turned back to what I had just read. I'd already recognized some similarities between Snow White's challenges and my own, but today I noticed that I had some things in common with the dwarves as well. They had been transformed by the love of the King, and though I had begun the process, I needed more of that transforming power of love in my life, too.

I thought back to our life before the "inheritance," and how our proverbial "American Dream" had vanished. Quite frankly it had never really satisfied. Always searching for something better, something bigger, something... more, and yet never truly filling the void. As I sat there staring at the faded words on the page, I felt an overwhelming hunger in my heart for purpose and meaning in my life like Snow White and the dwarves had found.

I considered myself a Christian, but my life felt filled with nothing but empty rituals and repetition. I, like the dwarves in the mines, worked endlessly day in and day out without anything to show for it. What had I really done besides warming a pew each week and occasionally opening my Bible to assuage my guilt? There must be more to being a Christian than this.

What would Snow White's King say about my perpetual striving that produced only occasional joy, very little satisfaction, and no real peace. Was it even possible to break completely from the past and experience the fullness of freedom or was it simply a fairy tale? The lie of the "happily ever after"?

Considering that last paragraph, I thought about my own faults. Could they really be changed? Most people just passed them off as "just the way we are." But this letter gave hope that they could be overcome. *Love changes things.*

Could I let God's light and love in to expose and heal those troublesome areas of my life? I mused, as I set the letter down.

CHAPTER 11

With church the next morning, I had no time for another letter. Thinking of Snoozy, Sneezer, Grumbly and Fixit on the car ride, I asked Mark, "What do you consider my faults?"

My sweet husband just looked at me and replied, "Oh, Honey, you're perfect to me." Then more seriously, "What's brought this on?"

I told him about the dwarves' transformation (at least the ones so far) and before I knew it we'd arrived. At church, I absentmindedly greeted a few people as we entered, my mind stuck on the dwarves.

Through the preliminaries of announcements and worship, Snow White's words "Love changes things" would not leave me. That inner hunger I'd experienced the day before only increased. Maybe others were satisfied with a mediocre Christianity, but I wanted more. I felt like Snoozy, getting a glimpse of something and starting to come alive.

As our pastor got up to speak, something shifted inside me. Every word flowing from him pierced my heart like never before. Familiar words, yet somehow new and fresh. "In this the love of God was manifested toward us, that God has sent His only begotten Son into the world, that we might live through Him." 1 John 4:9

As he continued to share on the power of the cross to transform lives, it was like a veil had been removed from my mind. For the first time, I saw clearly how Jesus' sacrifice on the cross, His love, saved me, Ann Richards, from all my sins, so that I could live my life in Him. A story so familiar, yet now so personal. How often I had heard this message, but now it seemed to penetrate deep inside me.

People considered me a "good" person. I did all the right things. But now I saw this wasn't enough. My best efforts were simply my own self-righteousness, which the Bible called "filthy rags." I saw in bold contrast to Christ's sacrificial love my life full of selfishness. Now I knew only the blood of Jesus could make me new, not my efforts or striving.

Pastor Paul gave a call for anyone wanting to re-dedicate their lives to Jesus to come forward. I trembled at this. I felt the tug on my heart. I wanted to say "yes" fully and completely. However, what would other people think? Maybe that I'd committed some great sin or something. I wrestled for what seemed an eternity. But then looking at what He had done for me, I felt His love and realized, "How could I refuse full surrender?"

"Love changes things," I could hear Snow White say again. I wanted more of that. I thought of all the different things the dwarves and Snow White did to work through their transformation. It didn't just happen. They had to make hard decisions at first, but found joy when they made the effort. I couldn't hesitate any longer, though my feet seemed made of cement, I commanded them to

move, step by step to the altar. There something broke within me as a fountain of tears burst forth. Embarrassed and yet feeling so free, so clean. No more facade. No more striving. Full surrender. A holy moment.

After a few moments, Cynthia, the pastor's wife laid her hands on my shoulder, speaking a simple prayer over me. No judging or prying or patronizing.

In that instant, I recognized the fear that had kept me back from genuine relationships with others. While desiring deeper friendships, fear of being judged bound me up.

"O Jesus, I want more freedom. Open my heart," I whispered under my breath.

Cynthia smiled and gave me a quick hug. "I'm praying for you. I believe God has great things in store for you, Ann," she said as she turned to pray for someone else.

A seed of hope took root in my heart at her words. Did my life really matter to God? Was there more for me than the drudgery of job searching and housekeeping?

A tranquil silence filled the car as we drove home. I was grateful Mark seemed to understand and give me space.

As the next week unfolded, everything seemed altered, as if viewing life through a new lens. I felt revitalized as if I'd tasted some of Snoozy's elixir of life. What had once annoyed me, now seemed no big deal. A greater peace took hold of me.

It wasn't until Saturday that I thought again of the next letter and the continuing story of the dwarves. With eagerness I sat down to peruse the next note.

Precious Annabelle,

At last I have a moment to spare, so must not keep you waiting and wondering about the other dwarves' changes. Where was I? Oh, yes! Dimwit's tale is a bit different than Snoozy's or Sneezer's. One evening I asked my King if he could cure Dimwit of speaking gibberish. Surprisingly, my King shook his head and with a chuckle explained that my friend was not sick, just a bit confused. "Dimwit has always longed to have an intimate relationship with his Creator, but has no idea how to achieve it. He believes the only way to talk directly to God is to speak in a "secret language."

"Is that true?" I asked.

With a broad smile my King assured me, "No. God speaks all languages, even Dimwit-ese."

Not long after that conversation, we determined to call on the mining dwarves to see how they were faring. It was a beautiful, clear evening, and unaware of our presence, Dimwit emerged from the tunnels into the clean, sweet air and began to make joyful exclamations using his garbled sounding speech. When the King heard this, he threw his head back and laughed merrily, then immediately responded to Dimwit in the very same tangle-tongued way.

Though Dimwit had no idea what the King had said, he felt certain the King understood him, and excitedly inquired, "How do you know the secret language? What did you say?"

Smiling broadly, my King explained, "I inherited the ability to understand the languages of all people from my Father." And in answer to his question he said, "You were praising God for the loveliness of His creation, and I agreed with you. But Master Dimwit, would it not be better to share your love for God in a language that all could comprehend?"

At this the dwarf looked a bit offended and explained, "I know everyone thinks I am stupid, or crazy, but the teachers who visited the kingdom the year Queen Snow was born assured me I must use these strange syllables if I want God to hear me and make me a better man."

"Dimwit, the God of all mankind speaks every tongue from every nation, and He understands your every whimper, every sigh, and even your silence. When you call out to Him to encourage your own heart it makes little difference what words or sounds you make. However, when you praise His name in the presence of others, would it not be better to use words they can understand? Then they can join you and bring Him glory, unless, of course, you have an interpreter. Why not reserve your special tongue for just you and God? It is your love for Him that makes you a better dwarf, not the language you speak."

Dimwit's makeover began that day. Those who had shunned him, mistaking his strange language for a sign of insanity, now recognized him for who he was, one fervent in devotion and that prayer alighted always on his lips. His family and neighbors now flocked to him when they were troubled and he never failed to pray with them. Though still delighting in bringing forth and sharing the great treasures from their mines, his greatest pleasure was, out of a heart of love for God, to intercede for those around him. I suppose you could say he became a true prayer warrior and an intercessor to the King.

Did he still speak this "secret language" to the King you might wonder? Assuredly he did, but now with much more understanding of the power that it gave him in his prayer life.

Merry's change was quietly profound in that he still smiled a great deal, but it was altered somehow. The King told me that Merry had the right idea about optimism, but lacked the knowledge of how to share it. He explained it to me like this: "Happiness and joy are not the same. Happiness is a fleeting feeling that changes with our circumstances; while joy is akin to love, enduring and unquenchable in the face of great trial. It is unrealistic to expect to feel 'happy' during sad and hard times, but we can maintain a joyful heart in all situations, allowing us to hope rather than despair."

In time, Merry grew to experience the full range of emotions, and most importantly, he learned that happiness is only a feeling, while joy is a state of the heart.

All of my precious dwarves grew in character and maturity, but to me, Timorous experienced the most astonishing transformation of all. After the dwarves began to find real treasure, Timmy expressed his joy by singing while he worked.

With only four of them left in the mines, he felt sure no one would hear him, but he was mistaken. One day while the King passed by the mineshaft entrance, he noticed the opening crowded with woodland creatures. Deer and rabbit, squirrels and pheasant, as well as a large number of birds all listening to the echoing sound of Timmy's voice.

As you might expect, after hearing him, the King determined to have him sing with the royal heralds. I feel sure that had the King himself not called Timorous to use his beautiful gift, few in the kingdom would have ever known the sweet, soft, beauty of his heart, or the deep, tender, love he felt for the King.

It makes me smile to remember how this once quiet and retiring soul became the most sought after singer in the land. As his love grew for the King so did his confidence and the once timid songster eventually became the lead singer of the King's imperial chorus.

With all the treasure they found, the dwarves became very wealthy and well able to afford a new home. This became a necessity as they all began to grow tall and could no longer live comfortably in their little cottage. Many said it was miraculous, and I cannot disagree. But I also believe that their increased heights were directly related to the internal growth of their character.

I loved to visit with the dwarves when we found occasion to do so. All our lives had changed so much for the better. We could laugh now about the old days and marvel at the growth in each of us.

I saw Fixit and Grumbly often as our paths crossed on the battle-field... Grumbly in the intelligence and strategy department and Fixit helping the wounded after a battle, but we all found love and comfort in each other's company.

It might be tempting to say that we all lived "happily ever after" from this point on, but in truth, life could never be what you might call "easy" in our realm. There were new challenges to overcome within ourselves and in the kingdom. Yet the overwhelming joy of being with our King made the difficult times bearable.

My dear Annabelle, the night is late and though I am weary, oh what a pleasure it is to share my memories with *you. My fondest hope is that through them you come to know the transforming power of love. It makes all the difference. Whatever may be your current circumstances, follow the path of love, and you will find joy.*

Lovingly,

Snow White

Hmmm. Once again I felt the enchanting power of her words of wisdom as I read this ancient gift left to me by my namesake. I pondered how the King had worked in each of the dwarves' lives. I wondered about the "dwarves" I'd identified at church and if it was possible for them to change also. This past week my eyes had been opened to what love could do. Could I help them find love, too?

I carefully refolded the letter and tucked it under the stack before going to find Mark. I found him propped up atop all our pillows, with one arm behind his head, reading a magazine. He looked totally relaxed and completely adorable with his hair mussed, and the cat curled up and purring contentedly at his side. As I looked at him my brooding vanished.

"Wanna go for walk?" I asked with a smile.

"With the prettiest girl in town? You bet!" He didn't

hesitate. Getting up, he tossed the magazine aside with one hand and reached for me with the other.

A long embrace later we were heading out the door and down the street. Though it wasn't quite spring yet, the day felt unusually warm for March. We strolled contentedly hand-in-hand through the neighborhood. With the snow gone, everywhere new green shoots of life appeared.

A group of kids rode their bikes along the sidewalk, dodging around us as if we were part of an obstacle course, followed closely by their ever faithful hounds barking wildly and grinning their doggie smiles. That old familiar ache for motherhood choked my throat as I watched them, but I refused to let it ruin this lovely day. I whispered a silent prayer and glanced up at Mark who was chuckling at their antics. To my surprise the pain faded a bit, and as he squeezed my hand I found myself smiling, too.

We sauntered along and talked of little things; the mild weather, the sweet smell of the air washed clean by recent storms, what we should have for lunch, which church service we'd attend tomorrow.

As we entered the local grocer's my eyes fell with longing on the bright yellow daffodils that filled a bucket near the register. Oh, how I missed my garden! I recalled our old home where flowers abounded everywhere. So unlike the apartment we now inhabited surrounded by a sea of concrete sidewalks and parking lots.

"Ah well," I thought, "we just don't have money for non-essentials like daffodils." With a sigh I headed toward the deli case, weighing the advantages of turkey vs. ham. Unbeknownst to me, Mark scooped up two bunches and tapped me on the shoulder. Giving a little bow, he handed them to me with a kiss. A little embarrassed, I looked around as customers who noticed just smiled. My heart fluttered as I gazed back into Mark's eyes and for that moment it felt like we were kids again falling in love with our whole lives ahead of us... no worries, and no limitations.

Reflecting on it that night as we lay in bed, I realized though still battling the sorrow that I would never experience the myriad of emotions and sensations of pregnancy, Mark was right when he said I was changing. Praying more and worrying less improved my overall outlook. I smiled thinking what a sweet season we were experiencing in our marriage.

Reaching over I brushed my hand across Mark's arm, my mind awash with emotion. How could we be going through such a rough time financially and yet, relationally I felt closer than almost any time in our marriage. Was it really all about attitude? Could how we choose to look at things make that much difference? With these musings, I drifted off to sleep.

The next morning I decided to take a little bouquet of my beautiful daffodils to church to use as a centerpiece at our regular Second Sunday Potluck fellowship. Wrapping the stems carefully in paper towel and covering it with plastic, I again admired the cheery flowers, hoping others would appreciate them as much as I.

Walking in to the foyer, I turned to say something to Mark and accidently bumped into widow Daniels. Apologizing profusely, I looked up into her usual grimace. I couldn't help but wonder again what made her so sour and grumpy all the time.

As if in answer to my question, the thought popped into my head that maybe she was just lonely and needed a friend. On a whim I decided to give her the flowers. You should have seen the look on her face!

She brightened instantly, "How did you know?"

Her smile was so infectious that I grinned back at her as I said, "Know what?"

"That today is my birthday!"

The face upon which a smile rarely alighted now glowed. I surprised myself by impulsively hugging her tight. "I hope you have a wonderful birthday," I said.

"Well, I sure am now!" she replied.

You'd have thought she'd just won the lottery the way her face lit up. I looked at Mark who was just as amazed at the transformation right before our eyes. "Grumbly, I don't recognize you, anymore," I thought with a chuckle as we found our seats.

After the service I sought her out and asked if we could sit together at lunch. As we sampled a bit of everything, from Amy's meatball casserole to Zoe's green jello-and-cottage cheese salad,[1] she surprised me by opening up and telling me about her life. She shared story after story, and they were great! She had me laughing one minute and nearly crying the next. I thoroughly enjoyed getting to know what a fascinating lady she could be once you got her talking. She kept thanking me over and over for listening and for the flowers, insisting it was the best birthday she'd had in years.

On the ride home I couldn't help humming softly under my breath. I'd never enjoyed Second Sunday Potluck so much. I found myself still smiling as Mark unlocked the

---

1   *See Recipes on Pages 175-177*

front door. I couldn't stop feeling astounded at the difference a few words of encouragement and a willing ear had made to Mrs. Daniels, and it got me thinking... Maybe I could find some creative ways to touch the other "dwarves" at church. Just thinking about it seemed to brighten my day. As I fingered the sunny daffodils sitting on our little dinette, I contemplated how I might engage "Fixit" or encourage "Timmy" and suddenly our little apartment didn't feel dark and dismal at all. At that moment it actually began to feel a bit like home.

CHAPTER 12

Changing the calendar from August to September I realized months had literally flown by since I'd read one of Aunt Annabelle's letters. It wasn't that I hadn't thought of them because as I internalized each message, they'd become a part of my daily experience. Love. Forgiveness. Overcoming fear. My once sterile and boring life now bloomed with new possibilities and I found myself busier than I'd ever been. Not a harried kind of busy, but the joy of an explorer discovering new territory.

As I more fully opened my heart to the love of God, I found myself growing in ways I'd never imagined. So much more fulfilling than the perpetual pity-party I'd once indulged in!

My mind wandered back to that moment of deciding whether to keep the letters or not. I couldn't believe I'd actually considered throwing them away. It made me shudder to think I could still be in that old place of anger, fear and worry had I discarded my inheritance. What I had once thought worthless I now treasured more than words could say. Not for the mere paper and ink, but for the life I had found in them.

Mark enthusiastically embraced the "new" me. It 'd done wonders for our marriage as the ripples of my change impacted him. It took me longer to notice, but it was true. A makeover was happening in Mark as well. Instead of discussing the weather or politics, now different thoughts, attitudes and ideas dominated our conversations.

Volunteering for activities or outreaches at church took on a new dimension, going from a "have to" to a "want to." Instead of something I did to "impress" God or get on His "good" side, I now participated in because of gratitude for all that He was doing in my life. Mark joined me as often as possible, increasing the pleasure as we found something we could do together.

One week at church as the Pastor asked us to turn around and greet someone, who should I find but Tabitha, our church's "Miss Sunshine" whom I'd secretly dubbed "Merry." She grabbed my hand enthusiastically and said "Oh, Ann I'd love to get together with you for coffee this week, please?" Before I knew it I found myself looking at my calendar and setting up a time on Wednesday afternoon. "Why would she want to meet with me?" I thought as I turned back around for the rest of the service.

Voicing the same thing to Mark later that afternoon, he joked, "Of course it's your magnetic personality!"

"Come on," I said, "She's way more cheerful than me and seems to come from a good family. What do I have to offer her?"

"That's a good question. Have you prayed about it?" Mark responded.

"Ok. You got me there," I smiled. What *did* I have to offer?

As Wednesday afternoon arrived, I'll admit I went feeling a little uneasy, anticipating her typical "Isn't everything wonderful!" syrupy attitude; but a surprise awaited me.

We'd agreed to meet at The Grinder, a local coffee shop that offered oversized wingback chairs set around polished wood-burl tables. A fireplace graced the back wall, though at this time of year the grate was replaced by large scented candles that burned day and night to add to their warm, welcoming atmosphere.

Entering The Grinder, I scanned the room but saw no Tabitha, so chose a table near the hearth to enjoy the flickering candlelight and a fragrant cup of tea while I waited. When the bell above the door announced a new customer, I looked up to see an unsmiling and downcast Tabitha.

"I'm so sorry I'm late. I just couldn't get myself together today." The words were spoken softly without her eyes meeting mine.

Though I barely knew her, I found my heart suddenly aching for this young woman I had often avoided. Obviously something was wrong. To my surprise I realized I'd like to help her if I could. After some gentle probing, she began to share.

As tears trickled down her face, she described a fight with her mom ending with her folks threatening to kick her out of the house. When she'd gone to her boyfriend to ask if she could move into his apartment for a while, he'd promptly broken up with her adding to her misery. What surprised me the most though was when she blurted out "I've been cutting again."

How could this beautiful young girl be cutting herself? Deliberately I softened my expression which I hoped registered sympathy and not the shock I felt. Tabitha's family appeared so connected and solid. With her bubbling facade, I had no idea of their troubles and would never have guessed her turmoil. I did what I could... I listened, and tried to encourage and console.

After composing herself, she turned the subject to me. "You seem different Ann, more settled maybe. Would you mind... I mean... I was wondering if you would tell me what or how or who has made the difference?"

No one but Mark and my parents knew the source of inspiration that had set my feet on the path of this newfound peace. Was it time to share with others or did I want to keep it private? Deciding to take the plunge, I blurted out, "It's all about the King."

Her eyes immediately went cool and her face guarded. I could almost hear her silent plea "Don't get all "religious" on me." Smiling, I explained about my "inheritance" and a little bit of the wisdom I was gaining for my life. Now curiosity brightened her face as she relaxed and listened to my tale. Glancing up at the clock, I was shocked to see nearly two hours had passed.

As we rose to leave she impulsively hugged me, "Can we please do this again?" she said, her eyes pleading. What could I say? I'd come wondering if I had anything to give and now I had my answer.

"Yes, let's meet next week; same time, same place." I replied, finding a corresponding leap in my heart.

One more week turned into two and soon we were meeting regularly. During our coffee chats I listened to the trials she faced, and then invariably shared something from the letters. Soon Tabitha asked if she could bring a friend or two who were also struggling, and before I knew it I was mentoring a small group of young women.

At first, feeling completely inadequate to the task, I wondered if someone else would be better suited, but the girls just soaked up the attention and appeared to gain something valuable from the letters. It felt great to know I was making a difference in their lives, and I began to look forward to our meetings. Watching them blossom as they listened and implemented some simple suggestions brought greater joy than I could imagine. We laughed and cried together. In a way, I felt my mother's heart reaching for them and their hugs filling up a little bit of the empty space in my heart.

As I grew in confidence, sharing with the girls became more natural. I enjoyed getting texts from some of the girls and experiencing their ups and downs which left me less and less time to think about my old disappointments – definitely a blessing. My past now seemed like a world away.

CHAPTER 13

To all appearances, we'd embarked on our own version of "happily ever after" I thought one day after church. Surrounded by a gaggle of girls laughing and talking, Mark and I neared the exit.

Pastor Paul surprised me by asking us to wait a few minutes as he finished greeting parishioners. The girls moved on, heading home. Stepping to one side, I looked up questioningly at Mark. "I hope we aren't in trouble or did something wrong." I whispered. He squeezed my hand reassuringly, but it did have the feel of being called into the principles' office.

I shouldn't have worried. A little later, with a broad smile on his face, Pastor Paul again shook our hands and said, "I've noticed changes in you both. Your enthusiasm and reaching out to others caught my attention and I was wondering if you'd be willing to host a small group in your home? We're looking for some young couples, such as yourselves, to reach out to new believers."

Excited at the possibilities, Mark appeared ready to answer in the affirmative. Tugging on his hand, I frowned a little and just said, "We'll have to pray about." Confused, Mark looked at me and then back to the pastor saying, "I guess we'll get back to you about it," as I started to walk away. Mark shook hands again with Pastor Paul and then followed me to the car.

"Wasn't that a bit rude?" Mark interjected in the silence of the car.

"Honey, think about it," I began, "Our cramped apartment, second hand furniture...get the idea? How can you think of inviting people we don't even know to this?

"I thought you said we'd pray about it. Sounds like your mind is made up."

Though I enjoyed all we were doing, this was just asking too much. I always met with the girls at The Grinder. They hadn't even been to our apartment. I had to draw the line somewhere. "What would people think coming to this "side" of town?" I responded. "Besides we do plenty of other things."

"You're ashamed of where we live? I thought we were over this," Mark snapped.

I could tell I'd hit a raw nerve regarding his ability to provide for us, but didn't know how to smooth it over. After months without a fight it appeared we were at it again.

"That's not really it. I'm just not comfortable having people over, that's all," trying to soften my tone, though doubting it worked.

A heavy stillness filled the car the rest of the ride to our dumpy apartment. Was Mark right? Was I ashamed of our circumstances? Trying to justify my position, I thought of all the good reasons to turn the pastor down, yet something didn't feel right.

Getting out of the car, Mark said, "Hey, I need to go for a walk."

Feeling guilty, I replied, "I'm sorry, Hon," and went inside. Restless, I paced the length of the apartment like a caged animal. Finally flopping on the couch, my eye catching the chest in the corner, but this time I resisted. Couldn't I have my own opinion about something and it be okay? Hadn't I grown enough? I didn't want any more "stretching."

I went to the bedroom to avoid the letters and my conscience.

I must have dozed off. The door startled me as Mark entered. Kneeling by the bed, he took my hand, "Please forgive me, Ann, for snapping at you. I understand you aren't comfortable having guests over and I accept that."

Now I felt even worse about my stinky attitude. He got up to leave and I grabbed his hand. "I'm sorry, too," I said, though not feeling instantly better like I'd hoped. What was wrong with me?

The subdued evening turned into a subdued week. How can I find joy again? I thought we'd done all the right things, asking forgiveness, etc., so what was still eating away at me?

As the next Sunday drew near, I knew I needed to do something. "Oh, Ann, why are you so stubborn?" I mentally scolded myself. Curling up in my favorite chair, I reached for the next letter, carefully removing the paper from the envelope and straightening out the creases.

Oh my dear Annabelle,

This is a letter I truly wish I did not need to write, but it must be done. It can be so easy to share the happy times in our lives, but much more difficult to talk about our gravest mistakes. Yet we learn some of our most important lessons through them, so I will endeavor to unfold my shameful tale to you.

Life, like war, is a series of battles. We had been doing quite well and had experienced many victories over our enemies. I had grown confident in my competence as a warrior, and gradually without realizing it, had begun to rely more on my own abilities than on my King. One day a messenger came to me announcing the presence of a small contingent of the enemy's army at the gates of the kingdom. Thinking I could handle this without assistance, I didn't take the time to summon the troops. For such an insignificant threat, I went to battle on my own.

The enemy immediately fell back as I advanced and it appeared an easy victory. Had I been wiser I would have recognized that their apparent retreat had been much too easily achieved. As they fled I charged blindly forward. A retreating enemy soldier turned at the last moment, raised his sword and grazed my arm. Barely a scratch, I hardly even noticed it in light of the victory. I could have told the King, or called Fixit, but why trouble them with such a little thing? I decided not to bother either of them. But by nightfall fever wracked my body. The last thing I remember is bidding my Beloved goodnight and retiring early that evening. After that I remember only a nightmare of confusion and pain.

As you might have guessed by now, the sword had been bathed in poison. The enemy had not been trying to storm the castle; they had been baiting a trap.

The toxin spread quickly up my arm, manifesting in ugly, red boil-like lesions. The pain so excruciating, I drifted in and out of consciousness for weeks. In my more lucid moments, I wondered why Fixit and the King could not cure me instantly and I sank into a deep despair.

I lost all hope of recovery and heralds were sent out to alert the kingdom that I neared death. During that time my King and Fixit rarely left my side, but they did take the time to send a special messenger to the dwarves with the news of my grave condition.

Timmy would not be parted from me, and softly sang songs of hope and healing over me night and day. When Grumbly received the news, he immediately left a strategy meeting with the generals to come to my aid and offer his advice about which oils and ointments might be best to counteract the poison.

Snoozy learned of my condition while on his way to a distant township where he was to speak before a large group anxious to hear the good news of his renewed life. He sent his companions on to the meeting to give them his regrets and returned to the castle to encourage me to grasp tightly to life and live. The other three all rushed to my side when they heard.

Dimwit prayed continually, and Sneezer soothed and encouraged the small army occupying my room. And my poor heartbroken Merry sat solemnly at the foot of my bed with large tears escaping his eyes. In his hands he held a bouquet of flowers he had made of gold and silver, and set with the loveliest jewels from their treasure trove.

I rallied a little as I saw each dear face gathered around my bed, and oh how

I wish I could say I recovered overnight, but that was not the way of it. More like an agonizingly slow process. However, little-by-little hope arose in me again, and as each day passed I felt a little stronger. Together, my King and the dwarves loved me back to life.

Six months passed before I could at last get up for short periods of time and begin to resume some of my royal duties. Once he felt sure I would indeed live, the King called me into his study. His eyes kind but serious looked deeply at me.

The questions that had burned in my heart for months at last burst forth. "Why?" I asked, "Why could you not heal me immediately? And why do I still have scars and weakness in my arm? I recovered quickly and completely from my stepmother's poisoned apple, so how could a mere scratch nearly kill me?"

He drew me into his arms and held me for a long moment before speaking. "My Beloved, when you ate the poisoned apple you were ignorant of my love, helpless and deceived. Because of that, my love easily and quickly overcame that poison. But this injury resulted from your overconfident pride. As your pride and confidence grew you became overly independent in your thinking, and chose not to summon me to help you in the battle. You not only chose to fight alone, you also chose to hide your wound from me rather than allowing me to heal it immediately. This placed you in greater danger than you ever were in under your stepmother's spell."

I longed to give him the same excuse I had given myself at the time... that I had believed the conflict at the gate was urgent yet too trivial a matter to bother anyone else. But deep inside my soul I knew he was right, and I had learned a long time ago that it did no good to argue with my King. "Will my arm grow strong and become smooth again?" I asked pleadingly.

Shaking his head slowly, he carefully took my weak limb into his large, warm hand and lovingly traced the jagged, ugly scar with his fingers. "No, my darling. The scar and weakness serve as reminders to you of this truth: You need me and those I place around you. Together we will successfully expand and defend this kingdom, but you can never do it on your own. If I removed the scar and gave you full strength, you might be tempted to repeat this mistake and

*that would prove fatal. Remember your
strength is found in me and in working
together with those who serve with you."*

*It was a bitter lesson for me, but
I share it with you in the hope that
you might avoid my mistakes. O my
Annabelle, flee from pride. It is such a
stumbling block. Be open to receiving help
from others. You need them around you,
not just ones you touch, but who touch
your life as well. Humility is always the
best path. Find it my dear, and there
discover a beautiful life.*

Lovingly,

Snow White

I agreed with Snow that this definitely wasn't my favorite letter. Yes, the forgiveness one was tough. But somehow this one left a bit of a sting, but I didn't know why. After all, pride wasn't that big of an issue with me, was it? I asked, not really wanting an answer. Laying it aside I tried to move through the rest of the day. Many of the other letters had brought swift relief and lightness to my heart but this one sank deep in my spirit, weighing me down even more.

Tossing and turning that night, I got little sleep and could barely drag myself out of bed in the morning. To Mark's inquiring look I replied, "I can't make it to church today. Go on without me." He simply kissed me on the cheek and said, "I'll be back soon, Sweetheart. Get some rest."

Sometimes I wished he wasn't so kind and would just call me out on my stuff. Have a big fight or something and get it all out there. But I realized that wouldn't solve anything. I exhausted myself trying to go back to sleep, but failed miserably. Deep down, I knew it wasn't my body that needed relief, but my heart.

Grasping for anything, even a bitter pill, I reached for the letter I'd read the day before, desperate for something I couldn't define. This time I prayed, "Holy Spirit, open my eyes to see what I need to see and courage to learn this lesson."

Startled, I heard a voice deep in my spirit, "Do you really want to see?"

Feeling just wretched enough to answer, I replied, "Yes." And with much trepidation, I reopened the letter.

Surprisingly the second time around was easier and as if reading with new eyes, I gained more. It was obvious once you saw it. Why didn't I want people over to our house? The truth – I was too proud. Mark was right. I was embarrassed of what people might think. With my expanding ministry with the girls, I wanted everyone to think of us as the perfect couple with everything we needed, not two desperate people barely surviving.

With the scales off my eyes, I now knew what I needed to do.

Getting up from my knees sometime later, I felt 100 lbs. lighter. Mark arrived soon after. Though still in my sweats, I said, "Let's go for a walk. I have another letter to share." I winked at him with a smile as he eagerly grabbed my hand.

A few weeks later, on a Wednesday morning surprisingly free of appointments, my thoughts returned to the "pride" letter. I'd been on a "high" these last few months enjoying this new life we'd found in each other and our church. Though hard to admit, I'd already succumbed to a certain degree of pride in "my" accomplishments with the girls. The conviction grew that even a little bit of pride was too much.

In a gesture that was becoming habit, I bowed my head and simply said "Lord Jesus, help me to walk the path of humility. Without You, I can do nothing. Help me to remember to live fully in You, continually giving You all the glory. Amen."

As the afternoon shadows lengthened, I continued to contemplate the letter. Somehow it felt like more could be gleaned, something deeper for me to go after. On this journey I was discovering that in waiting, additional revelation would come. Too often, I rushed through life, skimming the surface, missing the depths. Now a hunger burned in me for more.

"Patience, Ann!" I told myself as distractions crowded in and my mind wandered. In desperation, I breathed "Holy Spirit, would you teach me, show me, illuminate what you want me to see?" Then suddenly in my mind's eye, I saw an island - beautiful, but so alone. The missing piece of the puzzle!

Rooted deep in me was this need to be independent, to do things on my own, to prove myself. Ask for help? Never! Somehow I thought I had to figure things out on my own.

Though I now poured my life into helping others, I had no mentor myself. Snow White's letters were teaching me many things, yet it wasn't the same as someone in the flesh who I could discuss things with and hold me accountable. An island.

But how do you "unmake" an island? This thought dogged me the rest of the evening. Like Snow, I didn't want to "bother" others if I could do it myself. Now I began to glimpse my own need to have others to speak into my life. Determining to call Cynthia, our pastor's wife, the next day as my first step in seeking assistance, I fell into a peaceful sleep.

CHAPTER 14

For Christmas, Tabitha surprised me with a precious gift - a special place to keep my "inheritance"! A child's shoe box with an attached lid she'd painted to look like an antique jewelry box. As I held it in my hands, admiring once again the talent of my young friend, I opened it and read the words she had painstakingly written in calligraphy under the lid. "For your hidden treasure...your pearls of great price."

Removing the next to the last letter, I realized I'd been dragging my feet about finishing them. I wasn't ready for them to end. As I slowly opened the envelope, I felt a bittersweet pang in my heart. Gratitude welled up in my heart, but also sadness that the letters would soon be over.

Dearest Annabelle,

How do you put a life on paper? Many years have come and gone, each filled with the joys and sorrows of my life's ups and downs. Much of this letter you will not understand until you are much, much older and begin to experience the challenges of aging. It happens to us all, but I must admit that it occurred so slowly that I did not notice it happening... it surprised me. As my once raven hair slowly grayed until it became completely white, I noticed that I tired more easily and was forced to take a much less aggressive role in battles, and eventually even the affairs of our kingdom became exhausting.

My wise and wonderful King grew older too, yet he seemed ageless somehow. Nonetheless, he understood how I felt. He never pushed or scolded me. "It is a different season, with new challenges and new joys," He tried to comfort me.

I was certainly experiencing the challenges, but was having trouble believing there could be anything joyful about wrinkles and stiff joints. I longed for the days when I had boundless energy and could engage actively in life and in battle.

I hardly recognized my face any-more and found myself avoiding mirrors, even the King's special one. I knew what I would see....an old lady, lined and shriv-eled, whose beauty had faded away. I understood how the King had once seen youthful beauty hidden there beneath the rags I had worn long ago. But now my outer garments were the lovely coverings that failed to hide the withered woman beneath. Any beauty I once gloried in was completely gone.

At the King's suggestion, I tried to embrace an active role in battle through my prayers. I trusted my royal husband when he told me my prayers were vital to the outcome of the battles, but just as I started to feel that perhaps I was still of use to the kingdom, I failed at my duty. Right in the middle of a particularly important battle, I fell asleep. My task was praying, not slumbering! I felt so ashamed. What good was I anymore? I felt useless and could see no reason continuing to try. As depression crept over me I spent more and more time in bed seeking the solace of sleep... What was the point of even getting up?

One evening my King entered the chamber and sat beside me on our bed, "My beloved, open your heart to me. How I have missed your lovely voice and your beautiful smile. What troubles you?"

In a small voice I admitted, "Oh, my King, I have no heart for singing anymore, and I cannot find a reason to smile either."

He gently brushed silver curls from my forehead and whispered, "Why is that, my dear?"

With a sob I replied, "My life feels so futile! I miss the days of battle and glory. Without them I am worthless to you and the kingdom. Oh how weary I have become of wrinkles, white hair, and joints that rebel against climbing the stairs."

"Have you looked in my mirror lately?" he asked.

My downcast eyes spoke for me.

"Come with me." he said, taking my hand and gently helping me up. He led me to his study and took out the mirror. Oh, how I dreaded looking into it!

"If you could trust me in your youth to see beyond your rags to the beauty underneath, can you trust me now to see past the wrinkles to the incomparable beauty of your spirit and soul?"

I was not sure I could, but to please my King, I picked up the mirror and looked into its depths. So startled, I almost dropped the miraculous glass. There, looking back at me, appeared the most stunningly beautiful woman I could imagine. Although I could still see the wrinkles, an illumination brightened my face in a most breathtaking manner. I looked into my King's amused eyes reflected over my shoulder and wondered if I would ever truly understand the depths of his love for me?

Gazing adoringly at me he said, "You are growing more beautiful every day, my love." I blushed like a maiden. Then to my surprise he said, "Tell me about how your prayers are going while we are in battle."

Oh, how I wish he had not brought that up! I was just starting to feel better, but now shame swept over me again. How could I tell him I had fallen asleep and let everyone down when they needed me the most? I looked away and confessed in a small voice, "Well, in truth, I have not been praying lately."

"Beloved, look once more into the mirror," he urged me.

This time when I looked I was surprised to see the very battle that had filled me with humiliation. I could see myself praying in my room, and at the same time watch the battle being fought. Somehow, I was able to see how my prayers affected not only our own warriors but the enemy's troops as well. All progressed satisfactorily and then the moment I dreaded approached. I watched

the battle as it heated up and then...
there... I fell asleep.

I wanted to turn away, but my
Love said, "Keep watching." As I looked,
it appeared that even though I had fallen
asleep, my prayers continued to impact
the fight, and to my amazement they
seemed to be even stronger then when I
was awake. How could this be? I turned
to the King with questioning eyes.

"Oh my fair one, your spirit continued to pray, even when your body slept.
You are my awesome warrior queen and
nothing will change that. While your outward body weakens, your spirit grows in
strength, beauty and power. Remember
this, my love... never forget."

After that, I picked up the mirror
with renewed interest and determined
to look into it as often as possible and
to pray for each battle, especially once
I understood the true importance of it
(even when I fall asleep).

As I share this with you I find I feel
a bit foolish that I continue to stumble
like this so late in life's journey. I suppose
I imagined that by my age I would have
already learned all the hard lessons, but
apparently there is always something
more to discover. I continue to find new

depths of my King's love and devotion for me every day... even new revelations about myself.

Precious Annabelle, my prayer for you is that you will know how much you are loved and how beautiful you are. Age may change the outside, but you grow lovelier each day. Regardless of what you may think, you matter at every stage of life and from beginning to end, you are cherished.

I recall the last time I saw you, so tiny and so beautiful in your mother's arms. You were unable to do much beyond eat, sleep, and smile; yet, no child could be loved more than you. Please accept this truth from one who knows: It is not about what you can do or what you can accomplish, or even about your appearance. Your true worth is rooted in who you are on the inside. Remember, dear one, remember.

Loving you always,

Snow White

Though written by the same hand, and from the same heart, each letter never ceased to surprise me by its uniqueness and depth of wisdom. Maybe the transparent way she revealed herself in every line, or the love that poured from her King... whatever it was, these times spent caught up in the messages from the distant past were having a profound effect on me. This one was no exception.

My mind understood the concepts of growing older, but at 36, I certainly wasn't in the "grey hair and wrinkles" stage of my life yet. Hopefully, it would be years before I could personally relate to issues of aging. Yet the letter spoke so much more than just about getting old.

As I mulled over Snow White's journey, it dawned on me that it wasn't about reaching a destination--that magical "happily ever after" I'd always strived for--but about enjoying and embracing the process of life. My existence wasn't about getting safely from point A to point B. Somehow the ups and downs, twists and turns of our lives had purpose and meaning in shaping who we were becoming. In each challenging situation, I could choose either to respond in bitterness or let what seemed to be blocking me become a stepping stone to greater growth and ministry. I made a mental note to discuss this more with Cynthia at our next meeting.

The next morning I felt drawn back to this letter, again sensing that more lurked below the surface. Something about that last paragraph wouldn't leave me alone. An undefined aching throbbed in my chest, becoming more pronounced as I thought about it. I'd come so far in this journey toward love and, yet, I didn't feel quite whole, as if an ever present heaviness in my heart, like the weight of an unhealed wound festered there. That thought stayed with me long after I'd set the letter aside for the second time.

That night, I struggled to find sleep, eventually drifting into a restless dream... In the dream, I held a beautiful baby girl, her face creamy smooth with a perfect little bow-shaped smile on her pink lips. I gazed adoringly at her delicate features, delighting in everything about her as I traced her sweet face. Lovingly, I caressed her chubby arms down to her miniature hands and miniscule fingernails, then stroked her wee legs that were pulled up tight against her little body. I felt myself smiling widely as my heart nearly burst with joy. Then I watched in horror as my skin shriveled with age, and the baby in my arms turned to ashes that were soon blown away by a breeze.

I screamed and awoke in a sweat. Mark pulled me into his arms and tried to comfort me, but the devastation I felt wouldn't be dismissed. I lay in his arms for a long time, but the trembling inside my soul continued. Mark eventually slipped back to sleep. Grabbing my robe, I headed to the living room.

Like a light shining in the darkness of my heart, the revelation emerged that the wound in my heart refusing to heal was my barrenness. Though I hadn't actively thought about it for some time, I couldn't deny I felt broken... incomplete... inferior to other women. No matter what anyone said to the contrary, I still harbored the fear that my infertility devalued me. I couldn't seem to shake the feeling that I lived an unfruitful life.

Time after time, I'd tried to press down the despair of never being able to be a mother. But the desperate desire to feel the movement of a baby growing in my body or to hold my nursing infant to my breast always returned. I longed to experience the joys and even the sorrows of raising my children to adulthood. Yes, I'd also dreamed of being a grandmother...so many experiences that I would never know.

Covering over my grief with the excitement of mentoring young women had helped for a season, but tonight's dream... that vivid, beautiful, horrible dream made me realize I couldn't hide from this issue any longer.

Deep, wrenching sobs shook me as I poured out my heart to God...my only hope. I knew no earthly solution to this overpowering yearning, and nothing I could do would fill this void. No amount of ministry or stuffing the pain away could change the truth. I convinced myself that I must stare these ugly realities in the face, so I went to the mirror and prepared to deal with them head on.

"Ann, you are barren, and you will never have a child of your own. You are unfruitful, unable to produce, an inferior woman... a failure."

As I watched the angry tears wash over my face, a tremulous thought tickled my mind. "Do I really want to allow these words to define me? Is this who I really am? Is this how God sees me? Is my life truly worthless because I can't bear children?"

In the darkness of my heart and soul, I cried out to the only One who could save me. "Lord, speak to me! Who am I? What am I? Why am I? Am I being punished? Help me!"

Shattered and alone, I fell to my knees, crying out my anguish like a child. Softly, I began to hear a distant echo of the words I had read that day breaking through my sobs. "Precious Annabelle...you grow lovelier each day....it is not about what you can do or what you can accomplish... Your true worth is rooted in who you are on the inside... Know how much you are loved and how beautiful you are."

Even though I knew these to be the sentiments inscribed on a fragile piece of parchment, somehow they didn't seem to be coming from Snow White. It felt as if the King of kings truly spoke them directly to my broken heart. My tears of grief turned to those of relief as I felt wave after wave of His love wash over me, cleaning out the old wound.

The pain still existed, yet felt somehow different, a healing kind with the promise of wholeness to come, along with an offer to be complete in Him. In my heart I said "yes" to Him again, to this portion of my journey, and not just the joyous, fun parts, but this place of pain as well, knowing Him as the Tender Shepherd who makes me whole. Yes, I could let Him lead me through this "valley of the shadow," trusting Him to restore my soul.

Feeling peace in my heart, I tiptoed back into our bedroom. Careful not to wake my sleeping husband, I slipped under the sheets, wrapped in the arms of my King.

CHAPTER 15

As the months passed, and the seasons advanced from winter to spring, I felt new life take hold of me. My wondrous King had restored my heart to wholeness when He'd plucked that rotting barb from it, and the peace I now had was beyond any I could've possibly imagined. For some reason, thinking back on it now reminds me of my mother.

As far back as I can remember, my mom was the first-aid queen. Always quick with a kiss and a band aid, I could count on her to make all my boo-boos better. For the most part, her ministrations were painless, but there were exceptions. She refused to allow a splinter to go untreated, and she insisted on performing the "surgery" immediately.

Being a barefoot tomboy often found me seated on the kitchen table with my determined mother preparing to "doctor me." I can still see her holding a sewing needle in the flame of a wooden match, then wiping it carefully with alcohol. I knew from experience she was going to poke me with that needle and the thought of it made me wiggle and squirm. But as she held my foot steady, her practiced hand made quick work of plucking out the offending sliver, and before I knew it I was back outside, hale and hearty.

This is how I felt about God removing the "splinter" of my barrenness. Yes, terribly painful, but He wouldn't let it continue to fester in my heart. If I wanted to be whole, I had to go through the process of letting go and letting Him heal me of this painful issue, even though it hurt. How quickly the healing came once the "splinter" was removed.

Now finally free of the lies that had held me captive, I noticed that there were doors opening I'd never dreamed of. The small group of girls I'd been mentoring grew to include women of all ages and our gatherings soon became too large for The Grinder. We began asking the Lord to provide a more spacious place for us to meet. Cynthia, who had become so dear to me through our regular meetings for accountability, suggested we meet on Tuesday evenings in the church sanctuary.

Having the added room allowed the women to bring their friends, many of whom attended other fellowships. That led to invitations to speak at other churches, which in turn led to a surprising new career path. It still amazes me how the Holy Spirit was using my "inheritance" to speak into the lives of these incredible women.

As I contemplated His work in my life I realized the time for the last letter had come. Filled with anticipation and yet reluctance to see this journey end, I reached for the last letter. I held the envelope in my hands, savoring the moment, not wanting it to slip away. At last, I opened it and began to read:

My Dear Annabelle,

Up to this point, I have related my
life story to you just as it happened, but
I've saved one of my favorite memories to
share with you here, in my last letter. No
one can know how long their strength will
last, but I am content that I have left you
a legacy of love, and hopefully wisdom, to
help you in your own life's journey.

There has been much speculation
through the years about my peculiar
name. Many have suggested my name
is a reflection of my unusually fair
complexion. However, Snow White
was not my given name. My parents
christened me "Olive." Yes, I know, an old
fashioned name, but on the lips of those
I loved it was sweet enough. However,
on the cruel tongue of my stepmother it
became a moniker of disdain.

She would add dreadful things to it
such as "unfaithful Olive" when I failed to
complete a task to her liking. Or it would
be "untidy Olive" or even "awful Olive."
But the one that hurt the most was "ugly
Olive." It made me feel unloved, and
hopeless, and of course, hideous.

On the evening following our wedding, the King and I stepped out onto our balcony to watch a gently falling snow cover the earth with its sparkling whiteness. He took my hand and told me of a little known provision in the laws of the kingdom that allowed royalty to change their name at the time of their coronation. This surprised and delighted me. I could be called by a new name!

We stood there for some time discussing possible alternatives, but none of them seemed quite right. Our conversation settled into companionable silence and we held hands marveling at the beauty around us. With a contented sigh my King said, "How beautiful is the lovely white snow. This is how I see you, my bride, so pure and white, clean and bright."

As he spoke, the words "Snow White" dropped into my heart. He seemed to hear it, too as he turned and smiled, then laughed, declaring "My beautiful Snow White."

The day of my coronation dawned bright with hope and joy. I put on my favorite shimmering white gown, and tried to sit still as the servants attempted to do my hair. I must admit that I fussed a bit at them in my excitement to receive my new name and my crown.

At last the hour came. I entered the great hall filled with knights and nobleman, princesses and queens and joined my King at the front. He took my hand and addressed the crowd, "Today it gives me great pleasure to present to you my queen. Formerly known as Olive, today and forever after her name is "Snow White." This is who she is to me, pure, beautiful, lovely Snow White."

I stood there at first uncertain to the crowd's reaction to such a strange name, but not a hint of surprise or mocking arose. Instead, as one they stood and shouted "Snow White, Beloved of the King" so loudly that it seemed the very hall shook with the sound. I trembled as I felt all the awful ugly words that had clung to my soul for so many years fall off of me. I felt as light as goose down, and as free as a breeze.

Then to my surprise, scribes appeared with records dating back to my birth, and as I watched, they carefully blotted out my old name on every record where it occurred and in beautiful golden script replaced it with my new name. You see, it was not just a name for my present and future, but a name to cover my past as well. I stared at my birth record that now identified me as Snow White. Joyfully overwhelmed at this, I was little prepared for what was to come.

When I looked to my King I found him standing before me holding the most beautiful crown I had ever seen. Ornately fashioned from precious metals, and inlaid with every colorful jewel imaginable, it appeared as a beautiful flower garden weaved into a circlet of gold. He placed it gently on my head, then turned me to face the crowd as he declared once more, "Behold, my beloved Snow White, queen and jewel of my heart forever."

Once again everyone was standing and applauding me, one who was once a slave but now was crowned a queen. Staggered by his goodness and love for me, I turned to face my King. How could this be? I knew it was all because of him. So great was my gratitude that I wanted to take off my crown and cast it at his feet, but when I looked into his beaming eyes, I could see that my wearing it brought him such great joy that I just touched it and whispered, "Thank you, my Lord." When he saw how overcome I was by the whole ceremony he quickly dismissed the people to allow me to ponder all that had taken place.

As much as I loved being Snow White, I must admit it took time to get used to it. Sometimes people would have to call my name several times before I realized they were speaking to me, and then I would begin to worry and wonder if I really deserved to be called Snow White at all. Occasionally someone would accidentally call me "Olive," and as you might expect, I would cringe and worry some more.

As silly as this sounds, in those early days I spent many mornings standing in front of the mirror telling myself, "I am Snow White, beloved of the King." Gradually, I began to be more confident that I was in fact who he says I am. As I became more comfortable being Snow White, the less upset I felt when others slipped and called me by that other name. On the rare occasion when someone forgot my new, true name, it became easy to remind them, "I am Snow White" and move on with a smile.

Dearest Annabelle, I am so weary now that I fear I must at last say my final farewell. Yet I trust you know that your godmother loves you dearly and *that I pray these words of mine will touch your heart and bless your life.*

Did you know that the King himself named you? It is the truth. He chose the name that he felt perfectly suited his precious "princess." Names are very important Annabelle, and if you allow it to, yours can reveal something very precious about who you are to the King. Whether or not you like your name, try to remember that it reflects how the King sees you, and how he wants you to see yourself. That is all that matters. Cherish the name he has given you. Live your name.

Now and always,
your loving Godmother,

Snow White

Once again it felt as if Snow White could "read my mail." How was it that every single letter had a message seemingly just for me? I carefully set the letter down, thinking about my given name... Annabelle. During all the months of reading these incredible letters written to that well loved ancestor from long ago, my heart had softened to it.

I thought about my great Aunt Annabelle, her own struggle and her request that I be named after her so she could pass on the inheritance to me. And all the other "Annabelles" whose hands had held these letters, whose lives had been transformed by the words they contained. Though separated by time and space, yet the letters drew us together in one great tapestry. Our circumstances varied greatly and even our languages, and yet we were connected through the bonds of hope, joy and, most of all, love.

Unbidden, images arose in my mind of grade school and that afternoon I came home sobbing. Some classmate had teased me about my name and my mom tried to sooth me. "Annabelle is a very special name, my daughter," she said. "Anna means full of grace and belle means beautiful. This is who you are, no matter what anyone else may say" as she gently rocked me in her arms.

But in the moment, I didn't care what my name meant. All I could hear were the stinging taunts.

As a teenager, our conversations on this topic grew to heated discussions. I just wanted a "cool" name to help me fit into high school. Tired of the fighting, my parents had at last conceded to shorten my name to Ann, at least in public, which sounded more sophisticated and modern.

Full of grace – Beautiful - Is this who I was meant to be? Was I living my name, allowing it to define my true nature?

Now I realized, in a sense by shortening my name, I was cutting off the 'beautiful grace' God intended me to walk in. I laughed out loud thinking of what it would be like to go by Annabelle again. What would people think? Would anyone understand?

But then I thought about Snow White and the courage it took to go by a new name, one that described how the King saw her. Did God see me as beautiful and full of grace? What about all the mistakes I'd made? Ugly thoughts and words? How could He, who sees and knows all things, think of me as beautiful?

In my heart I heard the whisper of those words now so dear to me, "Love changes things." I could see Jesus on the cross, because of love, dying to wash me clean from all my sins, so I could be "white as snow" as the old hymn says. "White as snow," I thought, chuckling at the similarity.

I wasn't beautiful and full of grace because of the luck of genetics or my efforts or good behavior. I am beautiful because He makes me so. I am full of grace because He gives it to me freely, because of who He is.

A warm flood of His love washed over me as I felt His smile embrace me. Annabelle. Beautiful. Full of Grace. I knew if I didn't act quickly, I would lose my courage.

Mark was working on the computer as I approached. I lifted his hand off the keyboard and slipped into his lap. He gave me that quizzical look that I loved so much. With a smile I asked, "Would you mind very much if from now on you called me Annabelle?"

THE INHERITANCE

Simple Lentil Stew

Ingredients:

- 1 c. lentils, dry
- 5 c. water
- 2 tsp. salt
- 1/8 tsp. thyme & marjoram
- 3 large onions, chopped
- 1 carrot, sliced
- ¼ c. olive oil
- ¼ c. parsley, minced
- 2 cans of tomatoes, chopped
- ¼ c. dry or cooking sherry

Cover the washed lentils, herbs and salt with water, bring to a boil. Cover and simmer for 15 minutes. In a skillet, cook onions and carrots slowly in olive oil, until soft. Then add onion, carrots, parsley, tomatoes, and sherry to lentils. Cover and simmer 1 hour until lentils are tender. Serve.

Optional: place grated Swiss or gruyere cheese in bowls, ladle soup over the cheese and serve hot. Serves four. (This freezes well)

Ann's Famous Sweet Potato Casserole

Ingredients:

- 3 cups mashed sweet potatoes
- ¾ cup brown sugar
- 2 eggs, lightly beaten
- ½ cup coconut milk
- ¼ cup melted butter
- 1 teaspoon vanilla
- 1 teaspoon cinnamon
- ¼ teaspoon cloves

Topping
- ½ cup brown sugar
- 1/3 cup flour
- 1/3 cup melted butter
- 1 cup chopped pecans
- 1 teaspoon cinnamon
- 1 20 oz. can of pineapple
- Shredded coconut

Combine first eight ingredients. Pour into a buttered 2 quart casserole dish. Drain pineapple and carefully spoon on top of sweet potato mixture (may use just ¾ of can). Sprinkle with coconut. Mix topping ingredients and sprinkle over top. Bake at 350 degrees for 45 minutes, until hot and browned. Serves 6-8. Enjoy!

"Please Forgive me" Steak and Mushrooms

Ingredients:

- 2 lbs. steak
- Black pepper
- Salt
- Olive Oil
- 2 lbs. mushrooms of your choice
- 3 T butter
- ½ cup minced onions
- 3 cloves garlic
- 1 red pepper
- 1 T minced fresh rosemary
- 1 cup beef broth or red wine

Salt the steak well. Dry sauté the mushrooms (no butter or oil). Cook until the mushrooms release their moisture. Add a little salt and stir. Add butter, rosemary, onions, garlic and pepper. Saute over medium heat for 2-3 minutes, stirring often. Add beef broth (or red wine) and boil until sauce is reduced to half. Remove from heat. Rub olive oil into steak then place on grill and sear for 4-6 minutes. Turn steak over and check for doneness. Return mushrooms to burner on high and boil liquids down to almost a glaze. Serve over the steak. Enjoy!

Amy's Meatball Casserole

Ingredients:

- 1 pound cooked meatballs
- 1 cup sliced mushrooms
- 1 medium onion, chopped
- 1 large carrot, shredded
- ½ red bell pepper, chopped
- 2 cloves garlic, finely chopped
- 2 cups uncooked penne pasta
- 6 cups beef broth
- ½ cup each: peas and green beans
- 1 large can fried onions
- 3 tablespoons olive oil
- 3 tablespoons Wondra Flour

Pre-heat oven to 400. Spray 9x13 inch baking dish with Pam.

Cook pasta in broth till nearly done. Retain the broth to make your sauce, and place drained pasta into the 9x13 inch baking dish along with your peas, green beans, and shredded carrots.

Sauté onion, mushrooms, bell pepper, and garlic in a Pam coated skillet, then add cooked veggies to the pasta.

In a large skillet or sauce pan, brown the flour in the olive oil and season with salt and pepper. Add adequate amounts of the retained pasta broth (2-2½ cups) to the browned flour to create your sauce. Whisk until smooth. Bring to boil cook for 5 minutes, stirring frequently. Pour sauce over pasta and veggies, and mix thoroughly.

Cover and bake for 40 minutes. Remove from oven and cover casserole with thick layer of french-fried onions. Return to oven and bake uncovered for 10 minutes.

Allow to sit for 5-10 minutes before serving.

Zoe's Green Gelatin & Cottage Cheese Salad

Ingredients:

- 1 large package lime gelatin
- 16 ounces well chilled lemon-lime soda
- 2 cups small curd cottage cheese
- 1 small can crushed pineapple, well drained

Using the chilled soda to replace the cold water, prepare gelatin according to package instructions. Allow gelatin to chill until moderately thickened, approximately 1 hour, then fold in cottage cheese and canned pineapple. Place in a gelatin mold or serving dish, and refrigerate for 4 hours. Serve well chilled.

ABOUT THE AUTHOR

Adena Hodges lives with her husband and three teenage children in sunny California. As an Intercessory Missionary at the Rock House of Prayer she enjoys worshipping, praying, speaking and writing. You can check out her blog site at www.100waystopray.com. Her passion is to see Jesus lifted up and all to be drawn into the incredible journey with the King.

Adena has always enjoyed fairy tales from around the world and to see how God can speak uniquely through these stories in redemptive ways. She is working on a new book based on "Sleeping Beauty". Look for it in 2013!

SNOW WHITE'S LETTERS COME TO LIFE IN

Beyond Happily Ever After DVD

Have you ever wondered what happens after "happily ever after"? In this engaging monologue, an elderly Snow White shares her journey of going from slave to queen and everything in between. A kiss begins a transformation process, not only for Snow White, but also for her friends the dwarves who in the end discover true treasure with the King. "Beyond Happily Ever After" is a lighthearted look at the journey from slavery to becoming the bride.

Order your DVD today!

www.ingramcontent.com/pod-product-compliance
Lightning Source LLC
Chambersburg PA
CBHW032118020726
47494CB00007BA/2135